Voices
In Our Souls

Voices
In Our Souls

The DeWolfs, Dakota Sioux and the Little Bighorn

Gene Erb
and
Ann DeWolf Erb

SUNSTONE
PRESS

SANTA FE

Sunstone books may be purchased for educational, business, or sales promotional use.
For information please write: Special Markets Department, Sunstone Press,
P.O. Box 2321, Santa Fe, New Mexico 87504-2321.

Book and Cover design › Vicki Ahl
Body typeface › Chaparral Pro
Printed on acid free paper

Library of Congress Cataloging-in-Publication Data

Erb, Gene.
    Voices in our souls : the DeWolfs, Dakota Sioux and the Little Bighorn /
by Gene Erb and Ann DeWolf Erb.
       p. cm.
    Includes bibliographical references.
    ISBN 978-0-86534-758-8 (softcover : alk. paper)
    1. DeWolf, James M., 1843-1876--Fiction. 2. United States. Army. Cavalry,
7th--Fiction. 3. Little Bighorn, Battle of the, Mont., 1876--Fiction.
4. Surgeons--Fiction. 5. Dakota Indians--Wars, 1876--Fiction.
I. Erb, Ann DeWolf, 1945- II. Title.
    PS3605.R34V65 2010
    813'.6--dc22
                        2010023339

Published in

WWW.SUNSTONEPRESS.COM
SUNSTONE PRESS / POST OFFICE BOX 2321 / SANTA FE, NM 87504-2321 /USA
(505) 988-4418 / ORDERS ONLY (800) 243-5644 / FAX (505) 988-1025

Dedication

*For Erica, Dan, Sean, Eric and Mya,
our shining stars*

Contents

Acknowledgements

Researching and writing *Voices in Our Souls* was an enriching adventure, due in large part to the many generous and supportive people we encountered along the way.

We offer our most heartfelt gratitude to Beverly Neal, who shared a treasure trove of documents, artifacts and stories about her great-grandmother, Fannie, and Fannie's first husband, James DeWolf; to Jerome DeWolfe, a Dakota Sioux Indian who invited us into his home and told us the story of how his family took the DeWolf name; to North Dakota historians Vance Nelson, who showed us around Fort Totten and critiqued our manuscript, and Richard Collin, who offered praise and encouragement after reading our first draft; to Sharelle Moranville, a wonderful friend and writer who taught us so much about the craft and structure of a historical novel; to Carolyn Dodd, widow of Fannie's grandson, who shared her stories about Fannie and James; to John Doerner and Kitty Deernose who helped us with our research at the Little Bighorn Battlefield National Monument; to historians Henry Timman and Matt Burr, who served as our research guides in Ohio; to the State Historical Society of North Dakota, which provided microfilm of original documents for our research; and to the West Des Moines (Iowa) Public Library, which arranged our access to books and original documents through interlibrary loan.

All italics text in *Voices in Our Souls* is from diaries, letters, articles, books and historical documents. Excerpts from James DeWolf's expedition diary and letters to his wife, Fannie DeWolf, are as he wrote them, corrected only for spelling, punctuation and grammar. All normal text, including Fannie's letters in quotes, is the creation of the authors.

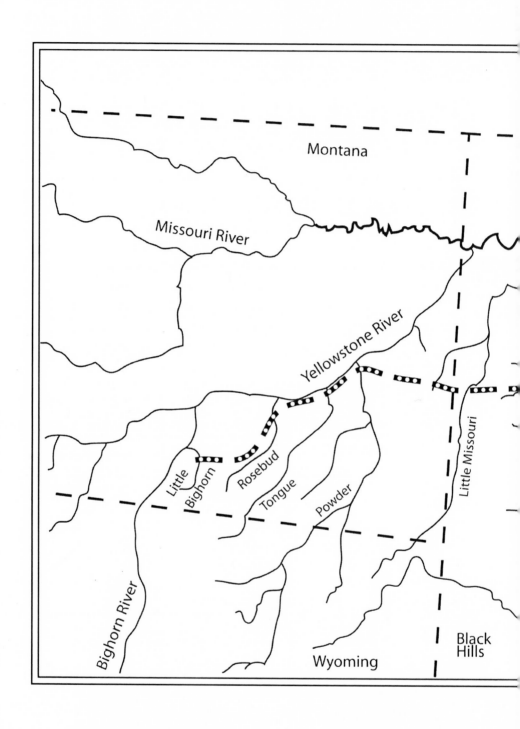

Montana

Missouri River

Yellowstone River

Little Bighorn

Rosebud

Tongue

Powder

Little Missouri

Bighorn River

Wyoming

Black Hills

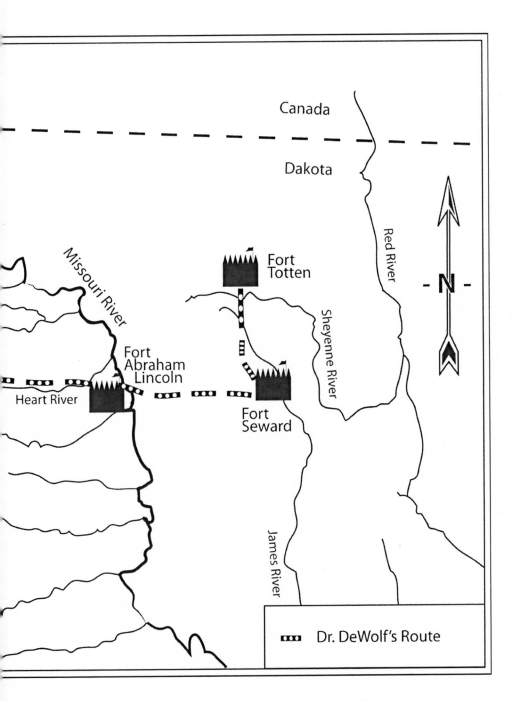

Dr. DeWolf's Journey to the Little Bighorn

1

Nov. 15, 1875 - Act. Asst. Surgeon J.M. DeWolf and wife arrived at the post late last evening in the midst of a driving snow storm having "travelled" all the way from Fargo D.T. by team a most unpleasant journey at this season of the year.

—Entry by Post Surgeon Doctor James Ferguson in official Medical History of Fort Totten, Dakota Territory

James stared out the back of the Army ambulance, a mule-drawn covered wagon with green-painted sides. The view hadn't changed since they left Fargo—snow-crusted hills with tufts of brown grass, an occasional frozen pond or stream, scattered clumps of leafless trees, brush huddled in ravines. Their routine hadn't changed, either: Get up before dawn, brew coffee and heat beans and salt pork. Eat. Break camp and start along the icy trail. Stop near trees by a frozen pond or stream, start a fire, brew coffee and heat pork and beans. Eat. Fill tin foot warmers with hot coals. Creep along the trail to an afternoon stop. Bounce over frozen ruts until twilight. Make camp and eat in the dark.

A mail carrier headed to Fort Totten passed them their second day out. A mangy coyote with washboard ribs followed their wagon for hours the next day, probably hoping for a handout, James figured. There'd been few other signs of life, no elk or deer, no groundhogs or badgers, not even a rabbit or mouse for that hungry coyote.

The mules pulled the wagon to the top of a high ridge, giving James an eagle-eye view of white hills stretching to the horizon. Awesome, inspiring, he thought, glancing at Fannie. Her eyes were closed, but he doubted she was sleeping. He wondered what she was thinking.

"Giddup!" Corporal Brown, hunched against the cold on the wagon's high driver's bench, lashed the four brown mules. Sheltered against the wind, James and Fannie sat under white canvas on benches meant for wounded soldiers. The wagon crashed through a frozen hole, rattling the few precious dishes, glasses and bowls Fannie had refused to leave behind.

She opened her eyes. "I should have packed more straw in that barrel."

"You should have left our breakables behind," James said. "I told you the quartermaster supplies everything we need."

"We must have some semblance of civilization," she said, sighing.

Fannie didn't say it, but he knew exactly what she was thinking. He could have left the Army and worked in a Boston hospital after graduating from Harvard Medical School. The Army had continued his meager enlisted man's pay while he was in school, so he felt obligated to serve at least one year as an Army surgeon. That's what he'd told Fannie. The truth was, while he liked Boston, he liked the Army even more. The military had been his home for fifteen years, ever since he'd joined the Pennsylvania artillery when he was seventeen. He knew his position and place, knew exactly what was expected of him. And now he had prestige. He was an officer and surgeon.

He wrapped his arm around Fannie and squeezed.

"Anyway," she said, "by this time next year, you'll have paid back the money we owe your mother and father for medical school.

We'll have our farmland, free and clear. We'll build a house and barn. You'll start your practice, and we'll raise crops and livestock and lots of kids."

"Campfire ahead, sir."

James peered through the wagon's front opening and saw pale blue smoke curling through bare tree limbs. "Pull into the trees, looks like we'll finally have some company!"

Brown spat tobacco juice and drew his revolver as they entered the trees. "Redskins, sir!"

James drew his Colt and checked the chambers. "Stay here," he said as he headed for the back of the wagon.

Seven Indians—a mother, father, baby and four older children—huddled near a fire in front of a lean-to covered with canvas and animal hides. Brown and James approached with their revolvers leveled. Fannie grabbed James's free arm. He shot her a look and turned his attention back to the Indians. "Peace. No trouble," the father said, standing with outstretched arms. His prominent cheek bones and coal black hair pulled severely back accentuated his hunger-hollowed face. He walked slowly forward, confident but not defiant in the face of the two guns.

James surveyed the lean-to and the Indians seated behind the fire. A rifle leaned against the back of the shelter—not within easy reach of anyone. A bow and arrows in an intricately beaded quiver hung above the rifle. A teen girl with smoldering hatred in her eyes had her hands under her blanket, but James doubted she was concealing a weapon.

Brown strutted like a fighting cock up to the brave and pushed the muzzle of his revolver under the Indian's chin. He cocked the weapon. "Oughta blow the top of yer damn skull off!" Brown spat a dark brown stream that ran down the Indian's buckskin tunic. "Damn red devil! Yer scared! Show it!" He pushed the brave's head back with the muzzle. "Cantcha even grunt?"

"That's enough, corporal. And watch your language," James commanded.

Brown stepped back, easing the revolver's hammer. The Indian looked at James and motioned with a hand toward his open mouth.

"Can't talk or even grunt, but knows how to beg."

"I said that's enough, corporal. Get some food, enough for all of them."

Brown grudgingly complied, and went back for more at James's command, then gathered wood and started a fire in a small sheet metal stove. "Beggin' your pardon for my language, sir, ma'am, but don't waste no sympathy on them Injuns," he said, sipping hot coffee by their stove. "They'd slit yer throat iffin they had the advantage."

After beans, hard biscuit and coffee, Brown filled three perforated tin foot-warmers with hot coals and packed the food and stove. "Them redskins, they're pretty much what you'll see 'round the fort," he said, urging the mules ahead. "Sorry bunch, but ya can't trust 'em."

"Been any trouble?" James asked.

"Savages held a big medicine dance last June, carried on for over a week in a camp off the reservation. Made folks nervous. A lot of 'em, like that sorry lot we just left, still roam, even though they ain't supposed ta. But they ain't got much fight left. They was whipped pretty good after their depredations in Minnesota. Wouldn't mind another fight, though. Be a pleasure drillin' a couple."

The corporal braked and jerked the reins as the wagon skidded down a rough, icy hill. Rolling over the prairie, Fannie fell sound asleep with her head on James's shoulder. Despite the constant rolls and bumps, she snored softly with her mouth wide open, then snapped awake when wind suddenly whipped through the buffalo grass.

"Ahead, sir! Storm's comin' fast!"

Dark clouds boiled high above the northern horizon, flattened at their tops and torn in white-gray shreds highlighted by the evening sun. The mules crashed through thin ice rimming the edge of a river ford then splashed into the middle where deep water flowed. The wagon tipped and turned in the current. James held Fannie tight with his good arm and braced himself with his other hand. The wagon leaned hard and sharp pain coursed through his bad arm; his elbow collapsed, and he rolled to the floor, taking Fannie with him. The mules reached shallow water and jerked the wagon up the far bank, sending James head-first with a crack into the china barrel. "Damn! Damn it to hell!" Fannie lay on top of him, her blanched face close to his. "Are you all right!?"

"Seeing sparks and feeling 'em in my bad elbow. Otherwise I'm okay. You?"

"Fine. You cushioned my fall."

"I don't know about your heirloom bowl, but I think my head might be cracked."

Fannie laughed, and then frowned.

"I'm all right, just a pathetic damn old soldier with a bum elbow and a big bump on his head."

She pecked his mustache and then pushed her lips through the prickly hair. "You're not old, or pathetic, but your language needs some cleaning."

Brown stopped the wagon, breaking their kiss. "You two all right back there?"

James scrambled onto the bench and pulled Fannie up. "We're fine, corporal, move on."

The storm hit with a fierce north gale that blasted stinging snow into the wagon.

"Slow goin' rest a the way!" Brown yelled.

The rumpled plain yielded to rough hills and timber. Snow chattered off the wagon's canvas side, above the wind's roar. James gripped Fannie tight and stared out the back, where trees and bushes floated like phantoms, receded and then disappeared. It took James a few moments to realize that one of the apparitions was growing larger. "Rider behind us!" The big man's lashed-down hat, black beard, rawhide gloves and long black coat were caked with snow. He touched his hat as he rode by, and then James heard him yell to the driver.

"Mail carrier headed for Totten! Think them mules'll make it?"

"Stubborn jackasses know the trail! We'll make it!" Brown yelled back.

"Who're yer passengers?"

"Doctor DeWolf, Seventh Cavalry surgeon, an' Missus DeWolf!"

"Be long past dark 'fore you get there! I'll let 'em know yer comin'."

"Much obliged!"

The light dissipated until James could no longer see anything behind the wagon. He wondered how the mules could find their way as he nodded off to sleep, then snapped awake when Corporal Brown yelled, "Smoke! Smell it? Injun camps! Gettin' close, sir!"

Tepees glowed eerily through the driving snow with dancing orange light from their central fires. James tried to imagine the people inside. He remembered Fannie's description of a band of braves she'd encountered along the Platte River while traveling by stagecoach to her teaching job in Oregon. The painted Indians splashed across the shallow river at full gallop, brandishing spears and rifles and screaming bloody murder. "I thought I'd spent my last day on earth." That's what she'd told him in bed one night in the afterglow of mutual discovery. "I feared for my virtue *and* life. I was sure they would kill and scalp the men and ravish me and the other woman on board in fiendishly devilish ways. At the same time, I couldn't take my eyes off them. They were lean and muscular, and they sat erect and proud on their ponies. After scaring us half to death, they demanded coffee and sugar, took our watches and jewelry and rode away." James smiled, remembering that night. He pulled Fannie closer.

◦ ◦ ◦

The fort's parade ground was dark, but lantern light glowed through the barracks' windows and in the windows along officers' row. Brown pointed out the hospital, a large, two-wing building, and then stopped in front of their quarters.

Candles flickered in the windows and lanterns lit the parlor, dining room and kitchen. Crackling fires in two stoves warmed the first-floor rooms. They found a brandy decanter, two glasses and a welcome note from the fort's officers and their wives on the dining room table. Beef stew, bread and peach cobbler warmed on the kitchen stove. James poured himself a glass of brandy after Fannie refused. They ate ravenously, James finished a second glass of brandy, and they went upstairs where they found not one but two bedrooms, both with straw mattresses, blankets and quilts. New blue curtains covered their dormer windows.

Fannie's eyes glistened. "There's so much room! After our tiny place in Boston, I don't know what to say."

In bed in their nightclothes, he held her close. "Fannie, I know our journey was trying, but I do hope you'll like it here," he said as he kissed her.

"I love you, James," she replied. "That's all that matters and is the only reason I'm here. I just hope you won't have to go off and fight Indians."

2

Freezing Waters Moon

Do you think I'm crazy to leave civilization behind and set up housekeeping on a frontier army post? If you say yes, you won't be the first. A lot of my friends back home think so, too.

—Rachel Foley, wife of Sergeant James Foley, answering a reporter's question at Fort Griffin Texas in 1872, Dialogue by Lisa Waller Rogers

Fannie feigned sleep when James nudged softly. After days of rising in the dark cold, she just wanted to be left alone between the straw mattress and heaped blankets in their cozy bedroom. He rested his hand on her hip and then slid it down her leg. Pulling at the bottom of her nightgown, he massaged her bare thigh and pushed more firmly with his hips. His breath warmed her neck. He planted a prickly kiss. She feigned sleep and rolled away. Gently, he persisted until, finally, he sighed and slipped out of bed. The hardwood boards creaked in the room and then on the stairs, followed by the squeak of the parlor stove door opening and closing. She loved him dearly and almost regretted her subterfuge as she let her mind drift through their past four years together:

She'd never known love before she met James. The youngest child of her father's first wife, who died shortly after Fannie was born, she was largely ignored while he lavished her half siblings with affection and praise. Her stepmother harangued her about housework and beat her with anything handy—usually a broomstick, belt or wooden spoon. She might be bruised, she vowed, but she would never be broken.

When she was seventeen, she answered a newspaper ad for a teaching job in Oregon. She asked her father for stage fare and he readily agreed, happy to be rid of the one source of conflict in his home. She was so excited. She would have her own income. She would be independent.

In Oregon, she learned that she would be living and teaching in the ranch house of a widower with three young daughters. He'd volunteered to recruit the teacher, provide her room and board and a classroom for his and his neighbors' children. She cooked, cleaned, washed and cared for his children. She helped with the ranch chores, too. After a few weeks, the rancher told her she must marry him to retain her respectability. "We will have more children, many boys, and bear fruit from the land and prosper and flourish as God intended. That's the way it will be. The Bible commands that just as Christ is head of the church, so a husband is head of his wife."

Fannie refused, and slept fitfully in her small room with no door lock, afraid he would come in. He never did, but she had to endure his constant, crude advances. An Irishman who loved his whiskey, he sometimes threatened her with clenched fists when she rejected him. She thanked God that his girls were too young to stay behind when they made their monthly trips to Camp Warner for supplies—two hours each way.

She was lugging a heavy box from the trader's store to the wagon when her eyes met James's. Handsome in his blue uniform, he took the box and placed it in the wagon. When she thanked him, he replied, "My pleasure," and tipped his hat.

She looked for him the next time they went to the Army post. Knowing he had a medical rating because of the insignia on his uniform, she made a point of walking past the hospital. As luck would have it, she glanced up and saw him watching her from a hospital window. Their eyes met, she blushed, and when she came out of the store carrying a box, he was there to help her again. When he glanced pointedly at her bare left ring finger, she blushed and explained that she was a school teacher boarding with the one of the ranchers who had hired her. Summer turned to fall, fall to winter, and then finally the next fall he asked, "May I come see you? Perhaps we could go riding, into the foothills or over to Abert Rim."

Fannie shocked herself with her reply: "If your intention is serious, if it is marriage, you'll see me as soon as you like."

His reply was just as startling. "I'll come for you a week from today."

The rancher was out "checking his stock" with his whiskey jug when she heard the wagon. All of the students, including his girls, rushed to the windows to see who it was. She told them to sit down and open their reading books, went to her room, grabbed her two bags and took them outside. The rancher's oldest daughter figured out what was happening and ran outside and screamed for her daddy.

Fannie shifted under the covers, luxuriating in the warm memory. They were married that evening under ponderosa pines. The post chaplain, The Reverend M. J. Kelly, pronounced them man and wife on Oct. 30, 1871. She was named hospital matron after the brief ceremony, and they were provided a small room in the hospital with a bed, chamber pot cabinet and night stand with a wash bowl.

For the first time in her life, she saw and felt beauty, even in the harsh, dry wilderness she'd grown to hate while living with the rancher. She and James rode several times each week. Sometimes they rode from the mountain-edge Army camp into the Great Basin—a high desert plateau with sagebrush and dry grass, broken by soaring cliffs and harsh rock formations. Most of the time, they rode into the mountains through park-like stands of towering red-bark pines and groves of whispering aspen. They walked their horses and listened to the birds' calls and rat-a-tat-tats. They chased rabbits and deer. They loped their horses through grassy wildflower meadows where pink roses flourished along sparkling streams. The fragrant roses were Fannie's favorite, and James always cut bunches for her to put in a vase in their little bedroom.

One fall evening when the aspen splashed dazzling yellow in the green pines, they climbed to an overlook and watched the setting sun ignite the land below. A high, black cliff extending as far as they could see flared bright orange. The straw grass and blue sagebrush on the valley floor caught the sun's fire, too. Fannie turned to James and felt heat when he kissed her.

They worked together in the camp hospital, setting broken bones, dressing wounds and treating men for constipation, dysentery, fevers and other common ailments. The soldiers' primary duty was keeping the area's Northern Paiutes at bay so the sheep and cattle ranchers could graze their stock in peace. For the most part, the local Indians kept their distance and left the settlers alone. And so the men drank and fought and whored, and then visited the camp hospital for relief from their self-inflicted problems.

In 1873, with Fannie's encouragement, James applied for and was granted a transfer at his own expense to the Watertown Arsenal near Boston so he could attend Harvard Medical School. They rented a small flat off Acorn Street, a narrow cobblestone alley where servants and laborers lived in the city's exclusive Beacon Hill neighborhood. There was barely enough room to cook, eat and sleep, but it was still more than they could afford on James's military pay. They borrowed money from his parents to help with rent and food and to pay for James's books, tuition and laboratory fees.

Fannie found a seamstress job with a tailor on Beacon Hill's bustling Charles Street. She started with mending and alterations but before long was making hats and dresses for upper-class ladies who would never wear the same dress twice to a social function. Their fittings were done in the privacy of their homes, so Fannie gained intimate knowledge of their households and lifestyles. Most lived in richly furnished multi-story row houses with ornate plaster cornices and ceiling medallions, lush carpeting, brass chandeliers and Italian marble fireplaces. Many had central heating and running water. The wealthiest lived in larger free-standing homes. Some were even plumbed for toilets.

Everywhere Fannie went, she was welcomed warmly, with an air of condescending kindness. For even though James was a Harvard student, he was not one of *them*, and neither was she. The class distinctions didn't bother Fannie. In fact, she was intoxicated by Boston's arts and culture, its dynamic commerce, wealth and energy. She saw unlimited opportunities, for her and for James, who didn't seem bothered by class differences, either. With the exception of a few students like him, he bragged, Harvard was the exclusive domain of the First Families of Boston. Not just the students but many of the professors came from what Oliver Wendell Holmes, Sr., his anatomy and physiology professor, called the "Boston Brahmin," America's highest caste in the city that Holmes called "the hub of the universe."

"I'm learning medicine from the best, Fannie."

She encouraged his enthusiasm, thinking perhaps he would leave the Army and continue medical practice in Boston after graduation. His studies were rigorous and his hours long, and she did everything she could to make his life easier. They rose before dawn every morning and while James dressed she revived the stove fire and fixed a hearty breakfast. If she could get ready in time, they walked together to the medical school, a drab three-story brick building on North Grove Street near the stately Massachusetts General Hospital building, where James and his fellow Harvard students conducted examinations and treated patients under the watchful eyes of staff doctors.

At night, she helped him with his studies, often reading and summarizing medical book chapters for him long after he had fallen asleep from exhaustion. She worked weekdays and Saturday mornings and did her shopping for food and household supplies on Saturday afternoon while James attended weekend military drills at the arsenal. They attended church Sunday mornings and if the weather was nice, took an afternoon stroll with other gentlemen and ladies through the nearby Boston Public Garden. Skating on the

Boston Common pond replaced garden strolls in the winter.

Fannie was so proud when James graduated in the summer of 1875. But even with his Harvard degree, he wouldn't leave the Army. So here they were in the frozen wilderness of Dakota. Reluctantly, she got out of bed and went downstairs. He fixed her coffee with a heaping spoonful of sugar and some cream, shrugged into his long, heavy coat and put on his officer's cap.

"It's that late?"

He nodded and pulled on his yellow gauntlets. She straightened his coat collar, fastened the bright brass button at the top and brushed lint off a shoulder.

"I'll see you for dinner?" she asked.

"I'm not sure, probably."

"I'll go to the commissary and trader's store and have something ready."

After he was gone, she dressed, fetched the chamber pot from its scarred wooden box, went downstairs, pulled on boots, shrugged into her coat and shouldered the entry door open against a hard, cold wind. More than a dozen white brick buildings stood like shining sentries around the parade ground. Men shoveled snow off the boardwalk in front of officers' row, where the quarters sported white-painted porches and second-floor dormers. The two-story barracks on the opposite side had tall, rectangular windows above long verandas and behind white-railed balconies. The centerpiece was the hospital, which reminded Fannie of Masschusetts General. Flanked by one-story wings on each side, the central two-story section was capped with a glass cupola. Smoke whipped from its chimneys, following cotton ball clouds, and the rising sun flashed gold off the cupola. Fannie pulled her coat collar closed and walked quickly to the back of their quarters, where she emptied the chamber pot into their privy.

3

Post Trader

During the war . . . sutlers damaged the morale of the soldiers with whiskey, high prices, and shoddy quality. In 1866, as a direct result, the army abolished the sutler's slot. Less than two years later, pressure from emigrants and isolated posts forced the army to reinstate a variation of the sutler's post in the guise of a military post trader. Once again, while the trader filled a void and made good money, he also caused trouble.

—"Peddlers and Post Traders; The Army Sutler on the Frontier" by David M. Delo

"**H**ello! Anybody there?" A woman bustled in, not waiting for an answer.

"I'm sorry! I didn't hear your knock," Fannie said. "You've been standing in the cold?"

"Not long. I'm Alice McDougall, wife of Lieutenant Thomas McDougall, the senior Seventh Cavalry officer at this post, actually the only cavalry officer here until your husband arrived," she beamed. "Thought I'd help you settle in. Missus Ferguson, the post surgeon's wife, wanted to come, but she's confined, nearly died in childbirth just over a month ago and is still pretty weak."

"Sorry to hear that," Fannie replied, "not much to do here, anyway. Everything's unpacked except my china. I'm afraid to see what the trail ride did to it."

Alice pried the lid off, pushed aside straw and took out a paper-wrapped goblet. "You packed well," she smiled, holding the cut-glass in sunlight that sent colors sparkling around the room. They worked their way through glasses, cups, plates and saucers until Fannie found a bowl decorated with leafy roses. Examining it carefully she found no cracks, and then nearly dropped it.

Alice took it from her and placed it on the dining room table.

"The china and crystal were my mother's. She died a few days after I was born," Fannie said," tearing up.

Alice put a hand on her shoulder. "Let's go to the trader's store. I'm sure you need some things."

"I do," Fannie replied, dabbing her eyes with a handkerchief.

They walked gingerly down the snow-beaten, slippery slope toward the trader's brewery and store—two log buildings joined by a short enclosed passageway in timber between the fort and Devils Lake. Fannie turned her ankle and nearly fell.

"You do have to watch your step, out here and inside with Ernst Brenner, the fort trader," Alice cautioned. "Nothing at Totten is more disagreeable than dealing with that man, not the isolation, not even the long winters. He'll pick your pockets clean and expect you to thank him."

The dark store smelled of damp wool, rancid animal skins, burning wood and sour beer. Two men in furs and buckskins examined guns and traps in a far corner. Brenner, thinly whiskered, pale and dandily dressed in a white shirt, black tie and gold brocade vest, stood at the counter near a pot-belly stove. Alice and Fannie hurried to the back of the store, where Alice tapped on a door. "That's the way to Brenner's brewery, where there's a room with tables, chairs, spittoons and a pool table. My husband reeks of smoke, beer and whiskey when he returns from that nasty place, not that he minds, but I sure do."

They browsed the shelves, which were well stocked despite, or perhaps because, of Totten's isolation—boots, gloves, hats, coats, flannel shirts and long underwear; rifles, pistols, hatchets, knives and traps; soaps, colognes and other toiletries; barrels and bins of sugar, flour and spices; eggs, milk and butter packed in ice; playing cards, poker chips, pipes, hanging braids of tobacco, and kegs of whiskey and beer.

Fannie measured salt, flour, sugar, cornstarch and baking spices into sacks, then chose four eggs, lard, butter, yeast and canned cherries. She added two bars of soap, a tin of tooth powder and a bottle of toilet water to her basket, and then followed Alice to the counter, where a young laundress waited ahead of them.

"Your account is two months past due," Brenner said with an accusing stare.

"I had personal difficulties, had to buy medicines and necessities I don't normally need." She was near tears. "I, I can't pay for everything now, please, Mister Brenner."

"Everyone has difficulties."

"It's just this one month. I'll make it up."

Brenner sighed. "You must give me all of this month's pay, and you must settle in full next month, with an added charge for my generosity."

The laundress hurried out.

"Such a kind man," Alice said, placing her basket on the counter.

Brenner held his tongue, recorded Alice's purchases and partial payment and then turned to Fannie. "You must be Missus DeWolf. Welcome to Fort Totten," he said, wiping a strip of oily black hair back into place in his receding hairline. "I trust you found everything you need."

"I did, thank you." Fannie placed her basket on the counter. "We must open an account. My husband hasn't received his first month's pay."

"You made no provisions for expenses?" Brenner's eyebrows arched.

She flushed. "Our travel here cost more than . . . "

Alice interrupted. "You don't owe him explanations."

Brenner kept his eyes on Fannie. "Officers and their wives are granted considerable leeway, Missus DeWolf, but there are limits. You must be judicious. Purchase only necessities until you and your husband have established a good payment record." He smiled. "I mean this only as friendly advice, for your own good."

He pulled her basket to his side of the counter. Taking items out and examining them, he placed some back in the basket but left the toilet water, one bar of soap, two eggs and the cherries on the counter. "You may keep what is in your basket. Please return the rest to their places."

Fannie flushed as Alice calmly reached across the counter and pulled the items on the counter over to her. "Add them to my account."

Brenner glared but held his tongue.

"Thank you, but you didn't have to do that," Fannie said as they stepped outside, "although I'm not sure what I would have done. I wasn't expecting that kind of treatment."

Alice looked at her new friend's red face and glistening eyes. "My pleasure," she said. "He did the same thing to me my first time. I hurried out with half of what I selected. He relishes humiliating people, especially women he thinks he can bully."

Alice placed the eggs and other items into Fannie's basket.

"We'll pay you, of course, before we pay anything on our account."

Fannie started up the hill at a furious pace, followed by Alice, who cautioned, "Watch your step!" right before Fannie slipped and fell, taking Alice with her. Their baskets skittered over the snow, and Fannie scrambled on all fours after hers, yelling, "My eggs!"

Checking inside, she hoisted one egg high and triumphantly yelled, "They're all right!"

They both burst out laughing.

Fannie filled two teacups and handed one to Alice, who savored the sweet aroma and sipped. "Delicious."

"Brewed with cinnamon sticks and sweetened with Ohio honey."

"You made an enemy today," Alice said with a serious look. "Brenner despises cavalry officers and their wives, thinks the men are cocky and it rubs off on their women. He hates me and my husband most of all because I stand up to him more than any other wife on the post. The one time he complained about me to my husband, he got a cussing and nearly got a thrashing," Alice smiled. "He complained to General Hunt, to no avail, which made him hate us even more. Now I'm sure he sees you as one of my friends and allies."

Fannie laughed. "I won't lose sleep worrying about what *he* thinks."

"Just be aware, he'll try to make your life uncomfortable, and maybe your husband's, too, if he gets the chance. He won't cut you much slack if you fall behind on payments. He's been known to spread rumors about people he doesn't like and has even reported financial difficulties to the commanding officer. Late debt payments can jeopardize an officer's career."

Fannie laughed again. "My husband's leaving the Army next fall. Mister Brenner can't hurt his career." More soberly, she added, "I'm more worried about rumors that there will be a campaign against hostile Indians camped in Montana. Do you think they're true?"

Alice nodded. "Word is, the Sioux and Cheyenne out there will be told to return to their reservations or face the consequences. If they don't comply, my husband thinks there will be a campaign next spring."

Fannie's brow furrowed.

"I wouldn't worry," Alice said. "The Seventh fought Sitting Bull's Sioux along the Yellowstone in seventy-three and sent them hightailing across the prairie. Last year, the Indians kept their distance when the cavalry invaded the Black Hills, their sacred Paha Sapa. They're not looking for a fight. My husband believes they'll scatter before the Army can get to them."

4

The isolated location of Fort Totten made it utterly dependent on whatever wild local goods could be procured, as well as whatever vital supplies could be shipped via vulnerable overland trails. Typically, isolation and the danger and hardship played havoc on post morale for officers and enlisted men alike with the resultant conflict. . . . Indeed, alcoholism and disease both caused great havoc . . . in the early years of Fort Totten's existence.

—"Soldiers and Sioux: Military Life Among the Indians at Fort Totten" by J. Michael McCormack

Doctor James Ferguson rocked back in his varnished chair with his elbows resting on varnished wooden arms and his hands clasped over his ample stomach. James sat rigidly in front of him in a ladder-back chair.

"A pleasure having you here, doctor," the fort surgeon said. "I've reviewed your record, your war experience and promotion to hospital steward after the war. I'm most impressed with your Harvard education."

"I admired surgeons during the war, working tirelessly as if every life, if not limb, could be saved. A surgeon did save my arm after my elbow was shattered at Bull Run."

"So your war experience inspired you to pursue a medical degree."

"Actually, I thought hospital steward was the best I could do. My wife encouraged me, prodded me, really. She even drafted the letter I sent to the Surgeon General, requesting my transfer from Oregon to the East Coast for medical lectures."

"You failed your post-graduate examination before the Army medical board, nothing to be ashamed of. Everyone knows the Army's been trying to cut the number of commissioned surgeons ever since the war ended. Even so, I'd encourage you to try again for a commission. You'd have a good chance with my recommendation."

"I hadn't thought about it, but I might, if Missus DeWolf changes her mind about moving back east."

"My wife didn't want the frontier Army life, but she's taken to it, or at least tolerates it. Your wife might adapt. As for you, I believe you will find your time here most satisfying. Having been a steward, you won't be surprised by our cases—broken bones and wounds from accidents and fights, colds and fevers, constipation, dysentery, liver ailments and venereal diseases. The enlisted men's morale deteriorates as winter progresses. They're cooped up much of the time, so there's more drinking and fights and, of course, more disease. They dump waste behind the barracks to save trips to the latrines. Disposing of horse and livestock manure, slaughter offal and garbage is more difficult when it's snowing and blowing, so sanitation can be daunting."

"Their diet?" James asked.

"Men suffer from scurvy if we run out of vegetables before spring. I've complained repeatedly about the bread ration. It's not enough for the amount of work the men do outside in the cold."

Ferguson leaned forward. "There is another matter. The Indian agency's physician resigned earlier this year. I'd like you to fill in until a new one is hired."

"Sounds interesting," James nodded.

"You could say that. The reservation's been in turmoil since

William Forbes, the man who established the agency four years ago, died last summer. Everybody figured things would settle down once Forbes's assistant, James McLaughlin, replaced him. The Indians favored him. All the officers here did, too. The agency's run by the Catholics, and McLaughlin was backed by the Catholic bishop in Minnesota and by Henry Sibley, Minnesota's first governor and president of the Board of Indian Commissioners. Everybody assumed the bishop would get his way. Instead, a man with no Indian experience named Paul Beckwith was chosen. He's young, green and overbearing, not a good combination."

"So why Beckwith?" James asked.

"Family connections. I think he figured he'd come out here for a grand adventure, study the Indians' quaint ways, convert and civilize the savages, and go back home. Instead, he ran into a buzz saw. The Indians despise him, and he and McLaughlin have been toe-to-toe from the beginning. McLaughlin used his considerable influence to get Beckwith transferred to another reservation, but Beckwith refused to move, claiming his wife was in a delicate condition and couldn't travel. Then Beckwith retaliated by firing agency employees hired by McLaughlin and hired his own men."

"So I'll be caught in the middle."

"You'll work with McLaughlin, so my advice is to avoid Beckwith as much as possible. It shouldn't be difficult; he's intimidated by McLaughlin and takes little interest in day-to-day operations. He spends most of his time in his quarters, in his agency office or in the post trader's store with his new-found friend, Ernst Brenner."

Ferguson shrugged into his coat. "I have some business to attend to. Feel free to look around. The Medical History Log is on my desk, and your cavalrymen's medical records are in the cabinet behind your desk. McLaughlin's in the stables. In addition to agency overseer, he's the fort's blacksmith."

James leafed through medical records and then sat down at his desk with the log. The most interesting entry involved Ferguson's wife, who gave birth to a boy on October 19. Her labor was long and difficult and from what James could ascertain, both almost died. Ferguson finally gave his wife chloroform and delivered their son with forceps. Nine days later, on October 28, his wife was still in danger, *her pulse being at least 120 and sometimes more. . . . Her temperature also remained higher than it should have been 100 degrees to 105 degrees.* Doctor Ferguson gave her morphine and quinine and she gradually improved, although her pulse remained elevated for an extended period.

James closed the book and stared into space. What if something like that happened to Fannie? What if she died? His gut knotted up. How could he live without her? He'd always assumed that when he was old enough, he'd get married, buy some land and farm near his parents' place. So he agreed when land near the home place became available and his parents suggested he go in with his brother Erastus and buy it. He told Fannie about the land after they married. No more words were needed, no discussion. They both knew there'd be lots of children; you need them on a farm.

Now, he thought the unthinkable: They could forget about children. They wouldn't need them if he stayed in the Army. In fact, they'd be a burden. In time, maybe Fannie would agree.

He put on his hat and coat and walked briskly along the parade ground boardwalk, out the fort entrance and past a steaming pile of manure near the stables. Inside, soldiers forked hay, groomed coats and cleaned their horses' stalls. These are the elite, James thought, men who charge at breakneck speed with pistols or sabers drawn. Now he was one of them.

"Doctor DeWolf!" Lieutenant McDougall greeted James from a nearby stall. "Welcome!" he said, slapping his horse's neck affectionately. "I'll show you around."

"Right now, I'm looking for McLaughlin. I'm taking charge of Indian health."

"Stop by the trader's store after supper. We'll tip a few and you can meet some of the fort officers."

"I'll do that."

The ringing sound of a hammer led James to the blacksmith shop where McLaughlin toiled in glistening sweat. With heavy tongs, he pulled a flat, round piece of glowing metal from red coals, shaped it on an anvil, shoved it back into the coals and stoked the fire, pulled the piece back out, shaped it some more, then plunged it with a steaming hiss into a barrel of water. After inspecting it on a scarred wooden table, he looked up. "You must be Doctor DeWolf. Doctor Ferguson filled you in a bit?"

"Told me not many Indians come in for examinations."

"Even with help from my wife, who is part Sioux and speaks their language, they're slow to change their ways." McLaughlin, a Scotch-Irishman with the fierce look of a Celtic warrior, spoke gruffly.

"Doctor Ferguson told me a little about the new agent and said most thought you should have been chosen."

"I'm more concerned about Mister Beckwith's rash actions than bruised feelings."

"What actions?"

"He's threatening to cut rations to nearly every family on the reservation."

"Doctor Ferguson didn't tell me about that."

"I tried to explain to Beckwith, we need to tread lightly. The Dakota Sioux here were driven from Minnesota after the sixty-two uprising. They roamed for years, harassed by soldiers. Many died of starvation and disease. The rest were almost dead when they surrendered in sixty-seven. The Army gave them food through that first winter, and the government continued feeding and clothing them through last year, even though they're not entitled under their treaty."

McLaughlin poured two cups of coffee and handed one to James.

"Last winter, Major Forbes and I told them all able-bodied men would have to work for their families' rations, beginning with spring planting. Half the men refused because they consider farming women's work; they're hunters and warriors. So there were hard feelings when farmer Indians received rations and the rest got nothing. The intransigents shot at their neighbors' horses and cattle, tore down fences and trampled and burned crops. We organized an Indian police force to arrest and punish the offenders, which created even more tension." McLaughlin slurped his coffee.

"When Beckwith showed up, I told him about the unrest. I thought he agreed we should ease up, but he got his back up and exercised his authority by sending word to the head chief that all ceremonial dances must stop immediately, all children must attend the Catholic missionary school, and all polygamous marriages must be dissolved. Anyone ignoring his orders would have their rations cut. I could have told him his demands would lead to an exodus, or all-out war, but he didn't ask."

"Most of the Indians are still here, aren't they, and there's been no bloodshed?"

"He hasn't cut anyone off yet. He's waiting for approval from Washington. I pray God they have enough sense to reject him. The dances and polygamy must stop. The children must go to school, but you can't push the Indians too fast and too hard."

"Tell me about their health and what I can do."

"Smallpox, influenza and cholera have taken heavy tolls. Many Indians believe we're using our 'white man's diseases' to exterminate them. As if illnesses weren't enough, the whiskey vendors take their money in exchange for acute drunkenness and chronic alcohol ailments. I've tried to get the Army to shut down the vendors; the soldiers suffer as much from alcohol as the Indians. General Hunt says he doesn't have the power to close them down. At least the Indians don't visit the whores, so venereal disease isn't a big problem."

"Why would they trust me, and how can I help if they don't?" James asked.

McLaughlin shrugged. "The grim reality is, a generation or two will be decimated by hunger and disease before they accept our ways. Take the children away from their parents and grandparents, teach them how to dress, speak, work, live and fear God as we do. That's their salvation."

"A cruel fate."

"In the short-term, maybe, but not in the long run."

"I'd like to observe the Indians the next time rations are distributed."

"That'd be Saturday."

"I'd like to tour the camps, too."

"Did Doctor Ferguson tell you about his wife and baby?" Fannie asked during supper.

"I read about her labor and delivery in the medical log, some minor difficulties, but mother and baby are doing fine now."

"Minor difficulties? She almost died, James!"

"It was not that serious."

"It certainly was. You think I don't know? It's one of the first things Missus McDougall and I talked about. You don't need to protect me. I know the dangers of childbirth."

"Okay! If you want to know, it worries me, Fannie. I don't know what I'd do if anything happened to you." He swallowed hard. "Maybe we should forget about farming and a big family and stay with the Army. The McDougalls seem happy out here without children. The Custers have no children. They live a free life."

"We're not giving up our plans."

"If I stayed in the Army, got my commission and some advancements, my family would take the farmland. We could pay back my parents and live quite well."

"Buying everything from fort traders? Missus McDougall said even General Custer and his wife live like paupers. As for the dangers of childbirth, you know as well as I do that we'll probably have children, despite our precautions."

"We might not have children."

"You know we probably will. Military life is hard for women. With children, it would be intolerable. Moving from fort to fort, no permanent home, living like vagabonds our children having to leave us for a decent education back east, that's not a life James."

"Our quarters aren't bad."

"That's not the point, and you know it."

James reached for Fannie's hand. She pulled away.

"Our precautions have worked so far," he said.

"Abstinence is the only thing that works all the time." She folded her hands in her lap. "Is that what you want?"

"I've been put in charge of Indian health," he said, changing the subject. "I'm touring the reservation with the agency overseer on Saturday."

"I'd like to go along."

James frowned. "I'm not sure it would be proper."

"General Custer's wife goes everywhere with him. Alice McDougall told me she rides right next to her husband. Sometimes other wives join her."

"Rank has its privileges."

"With my nursing experience, you know I'd be of help. I need something to do, more than a little volunteer work at the hospital."

"I have to go." James pushed away from the table. "Tom McDougall wants me to meet some of the other officers at the trader's store."

"Don't drink too much."

James rolled his eyes on his way out the door.

● ◦ ● ◦ ●

The smoky room in Brenner's brewery stunk of sour beer mash and whiskey, and it was so noisy, James had to shout to be heard. He sipped whiskey but declined billiards and poker, knowing Fannie would be furious if he lost any money. By midnight, he knew the words to one verse and the roaring chorus of *Garryowen*, the Seventh Cavalry's rallying song:

The verse:

Our hearts so stout have got us fame,
For soon t'is known from whence we came
Where're we go they dread the name
Of Garryowen in glory

And then the rousing chorus:

Instead of Spa we'll drink down ale,
And pay the reck'ning on the nail;
No man for debt shall go to jail
From Garryowen in glory

He looked around and tried to remember the names and duties of the officers. A handsome young fellow headed his way: "Captain Harbach?" he shouted over the din.

"Right!" Harbach grinned.

"With the Twentieth Infantry!"

"Right again!" Harbach wrapped his arm around James's shoulder. "I saw your wife walking with Missus McDougall. She's a most attractive woman."

"I don't disagree!"

"Here's a toast to you, Doc, and to your lovely wife." Harbach drained his shot glass. "A young woman such as yours is as rare as the most precious of stones out here. May she warm your nights and brighten our days!"

◇ ◦ ◇

Around 2 a.m., James found himself singing and staggering down the fort's slippery boardwalk. McDougall veered left. "C'mon, Doc, gotta relieve yourself before you get to your quarters!" James followed and McDougall yelled, "Whatever you do, stop singing Custer's song before you go inside."

They staggered back to the boardwalk and past Brevet General Lewis Cass Hunt's quarters, their words to *Garryowen* echoing off the brick walls. By the time James reached his quarters, he'd sobered enough to quiet his singing, but he couldn't get the infectious tune out of his head. He mumbled the words as he stumbled through the front door and up the stairs to their bedroom. Sitting on the edge of their bed, he heard Fannie behind him.

"Liquor speaks the words of a fool, James. You have humiliated me and yourself." Her angry voice stabbed him through the darkness. She turned away when he climbed into bed. He was alone when he awoke with a pounding headache. He dressed and went downstairs. Fannie brought him a biscuit and coffee.

"Never again, James, I don't mind an occasional drink, but I won't tolerate a drunkard." James nibbled at the biscuit and sipped the coffee. When his cup was empty, Fannie refilled it. "Drink it and then go to the hospital." She gently squeezed his shoulder and went back to the kitchen.

5

White Medicine

Reservations could be policed by well-situated military posts, so that the process of adjusting and educating the Indian to the white man's way of life could begin in earnest. It appeared that this process might indeed be less difficult as a result of the widespread destitution of the Sioux caused by cancellation of land rights and annuities in the wake of the Great Sioux Uprising [of 1862 in Minnesota].

—"Soldiers and Sioux: Military Life Among the Indians at Fort Totten" by J. Michael McCormack

The four riders reined their horses on a rise above the frozen lake and watched Indians join a growing line in front of one of the old fort's log buildings.

"The Sioux here are Wahpeton, Sisseton and Cuthead. That's Little Fish, their head chief," McLaughlin said, pointing at a dignified-looking man near the head of the line. "We'll ride to his camp after you've had a chance to look around here."

McLaughlin kneed his horse toward a hitching rail in front of the two-story building. James followed but Fannie tarried, fascinated by a dark-eyed boy squirming in the arms of a young woman standing next to Little Fish. The boy stretched toward the chief with hands clasped so tightly his little knuckles yellowed. His mother relented and handed the boy into the chief's waiting arms.

"The boy's mother is Little Fish's daughter-in-law," McLaughlin's wife, Marie, told Fannie. "Her Sioux name means Gives To Her Brothers, but she's also called Walks Behind because when she was younger, traveling with her family, she would stop to harvest herbs and berries, pick flowers and collect pretty stones."

"Fannie!" James yelled impatiently as he and McLaughlin tied their horses. He instantly felt bad, realizing that it was the Indians' sad condition that had fouled his mood. McLaughlin went inside but James waited.

"Little Fish's wife has been very sick," he heard Marie telling Fannie as they tied their horses. "It worries me that she isn't with them today."

Inside, McLaughlin took them into a dimly lit room with shelves loaded with moth-eaten blankets, used clothing and bags of flour, coffee, sugar and cured meat. "The Army turned the old Fort Totten over to the agency after the new one was finished. We have more than enough provisions here to last through the winter. In fact, with so many men refusing to do farm work for their rations, we have a substantial surplus at the end of ration days."

"What happens to the excess?" James asked.

"Some goes to our most destitute, frail and elderly Indians who can't work. The rest is turned over to the fort trader," McLaughlin replied.

Fannie flushed. "So what the newspapers report is true. The more the agencies hold back, the more fort traders profit."

"Fannie, this isn't the time," James said.

"It's all right, Doctor," McLaughlin interjected. "The Interior Secretary has directed that all undistributed rations must be sent to the nearest fort trader. There may be corruption at some agencies, Missus DeWolf, but we follow the rules here."

"That's what I'm saying. The rules are part of the . . ."

"Fannie, hold your tongue!" James turned to McLaughlin.

"I'm sorry for the interruption. You didn't mention potatoes or vegetables."

"The Indians grow and preserve their own," McLaughlin replied.

"And haven't had much for several years because of drought, beetles and grasshoppers," Marie quickly added.

They went back outside, where Indians were departing with their goods while others joined the growing line.

"There are just over a thousand Indians here, most slow to change their ways," McLaughlin said.

"Some of their ways work better for them than ours." Marie started to say more, but her husband cut her off.

"We'll tour the camps now!"

They mounted and followed McLaughlin through snowy fields to cabins and tepees huddled in a valley. Smoke sifted through bare trees. Ponies nipped at brown stubble. Two children played near a fire where their mother tended a steaming kettle.

"I'm sure you've noticed the trails from their dwellings into the brush," McLaughlin said to James. "I've told them to dig pits for their waste, but they say the white men's smelly houses are disgusting."

"The ground around their dwellings looks clean. What do they do with their garbage?" James asked.

"They use just about everything. What little is left is cleaned up by their dogs and scavengers."

McLaughlin kneed his horse. "We'll visit Chief Little Fish first. He's expecting us, so he'll be decked out in his headdress and finest buckskins. Like most of the Indians here, he still lives in a tepee."

"I've never seen Indians in their natural home!" Fannie said.

"The old ways and dress are interesting to visitors, Missus DeWolf, but they're not to the benefit of the Indian," McLaughlin replied.

They rode up a frozen stream to the foot of a hill, where Little Fish's brightly painted tepee stood next to a small clump of trees. Red triangles circled the bottom of the dwelling; a black ring with white triangles circled the top. Scenes of mounted warriors dashing after buffalo filled the space in between.

They tied their horses to a corral's split rail fence as a young woman came out to greet them. It was warm and roomy inside. The hard-packed dirt floor was circled with blankets and buffalo hides. Smoke curled to the open peak from the center fire. Little Fish sat crossed-legged on hides, dressed in a deerskin tunic and pants decorated with finely beaded green leaves and colorful flowers. He motioned for his guests to sit and said, "Koda Waste."

"His words mean 'friend, good,'" Marie said.

Little Fish spoke again and Marie translated. "He says you are welcome in the camps of Mni Wakan Oyate, the Spirit Lake Dakota." Marie told Little Fish that Doctor DeWolf wanted to help his people with white medicine. Little Fish spoke and she translated: "He says, 'We have our own medicine and our own medicine men.'"

"Tell him I can see from his face, and from the faces of many others, that he and his people have suffered from our smallpox. White men have brought many bad diseases to his people. That is why they need white men's medicine," James said.

Marie spoke to the chief in Dakota.

Little Fish closed his eyes, bowed his head and thought of the people who died during their years of flight and wandering. Most of the old people died, many babies died, too. Healthy young children and adults succumbed to starvation and the scarring disease the whites called smallpox. He was one of many survivors who carried its marks. They ate roots and even the grass one of the white traders in Minnesota once said they should eat. They gorged themselves when they found a buffalo herd and were lucky enough to kill a few. It was hard chasing and killing them, for their horses were as hungry as they were, and they had only a few working rifles and little ammunition. Constantly chased and harassed by the bluecoats, they couldn't rest in peace and replenish their arrows. They seldom had time to dry meat or make pemmican.

He kept his head bowed, seemingly oblivious to his visitors. Finally, he looked directly at James. "Your diseases have taken many of our people. They confound our medicine," Marie translated, and then Little Fish spoke in English: "The white man named for the wolf is welcome."

"Where is Wenonah?" Marie asked Little Fish.

Grief overcame the chief's time-ravaged face. He spoke softly and Marie translated. "His wife has gone off with Walks Behind and her daughters to a lone tepee away from the camps. Her coughing disease has grown much worse. She wants to die in the traditional way and doesn't want to be forced to move into a white man's dwelling."

<hr />

Fat flakes flurried through soft air and melted on James's face. Closing his eyes, he felt his horse's rhythmic strides and imagined himself floating above the snowy hills, looking down at their passage—four dark dots on a white, rumpled quilt. He opened his eyes and looked at Fannie, who appeared lost in her own world. How could he be so lucky? She not only loved him, she believed in him as no one else ever had. And so now he was a doctor.

Harsh barks snapped him from his reverie. Cresting a hill, he saw the source of the sound below—a blanket-bundled woman sitting outside a white canvas tepee.

"Wenonah!" Marie shouted as they drew close and the woman's thin body convulsed in another round of gasps, wheezes and barks. They conversed for several minutes in Dakota, and then Marie told James in English: "You can examine her. She has consented, only because she and I are friends."

"How long has she has been ill?" James asked.

Marie spoke Dakota and translated Wenonah's reply. "A few weeks ago, her body grew hot but she couldn't stay warm. Her head and bones ache now. She can't stop coughing. She sent the medicine man away and is waiting for the spirit world."

James squatted close and looked into Wenonah's dead eyes. "What did the medicine man do for her?"

Marie translated, "He gave her root tea and kept her by the fire in her tepee. Walks Behind and her daughters care for her now. Her son, Arousing Hawk, brings firewood."

"What they're doing is good," James said, "but she needs aggressive treatment now. I think she fell ill with influenza, and now she has whooping cough, too."

"She should be moved to a cabin or to a bed at the agency," McLaughlin said.

Wenonah barked and hacked up bloody green sputum. James looked up at McLaughlin. "If this is where she's comfortable, she should stay here." He turned to Marie. "Tell her I will treat her in her tepee, unless she'd rather move to a cabin or agency bed."

Wenonah smiled and spoke. "She says if you'd tried to move her, she would have sent you away."

"I'll need quinine to break her fever and ingredients for a cough syrup, poultice and stew. Can the agency provide these things?" James asked McLaughlin.

"The medication, yes, but her family must provide the food."

"We'll need vegetables and meat for the stew. Onions simmered in sugar water will do for the cough syrup. Missus McClaughlin, would you ask the young woman if her family can provide these things?" James asked.

Walks Behind looked down at the baby cradled in her arms and shook her head.

"Their rations are almost gone. There hasn't been enough work to buy much more."

"This woman will die if you don't provide the food," James told McLaughlin.

"That's not possible. Her family's not destitute."

James turned beet red and stabbed a finger at Walks Behind. "Look at her! Do you see how thin she is?" He gestured toward Wenonah. "You don't agree she needs food?"

"Her family has able-bodied men. *They* must provide for her."

"You heard! There's not enough work!" A vein popped on James's high forehead. "You must provide what I need. Furthermore, I intend to conduct a health census that will demonstrate the widespread destitution and malnutrition here."

McLaughlin flushed. "You don't understand the government's

definition of destitute, doctor. It includes only the most elderly and frail who cannot work."

"Provide the food or I'll tell my superiors I can't work with the agency."

McLaughlin sighed. "You'll get what you need, but only for her. Conduct your census, for all the good it will do." He turned his horse and rode off toward the fort.

○ ○ ○

James, Fannie and Marie rode back with the supplies that afternoon. On their way, Marie said, "Wenonah is highly regarded, partly because she's a chief's wife but mostly because of the fine example she sets for all Dakota women. Her name describes a woman who is charitable and kind, who has a tepee where everyone is welcome. She takes pride in the fact that Chief Little Fish's Dakota name is Tiowaste, which means Good Lodge."

Marie and Walks Behind started the stew and then Fannie showed Walks Behind how to make and apply the poultice without blistering Wenonah's skin.

"I intend to conduct examinations in the camps from now on. I'll need both of you to assist me," James told them on their way back to the fort.

That night, Fannie said, "I'm proud, the way you stood up to McLaughlin today. But don't ever scold me again, the way you did when I was questioning him about the agency's surplus goods."

"We have to tread lightly, Fannie. It won't do any good to make enemies."

○ ○ ○

James, Fannie and Marie visited the Indian camps two or three times a week to gather health and nutrition information. Their frequent visits, and James's willingness to come to them for examinations, impressed the Spirit Lake Dakota. Scores lined up with complaints of ailments. Many listened, too, when James told them he knew the privies smelled bad but using them would help keep white men's diseases away.

"Use waste pots if you don't want to sit inside. Empty the pots into the pits and scrub the pots and your hands with soap and clean water. Keep your cabins as clean as your tepees. If you do these things, the white men's diseases won't harm so many."

The stew and cough syrup soothed Wenonah's throat and allowed her more rest. One day she said, "Your medicine has chased your people's bad spirits. The ghosts no longer call me." When she was well enough, she spread the word: "Doctor DeWolf is a healer. He saved my life. He can save our people from white men's diseases."

◆ ◇ ◆ ◇

James presented his findings to McLaughlin when the census was completed. "Over a third of the Indians, roughly three hundred and fifty, are severely malnourished. That's more than four times the number of Indians who receive rations because they're considered destitute."

"Take it to Beckwith. It's not within my power to do anything."

James tried for several days to meet with Beckwith. When he went to the agent's office, Beckwith either wasn't in or was hiding behind his locked door. When he visited the agent's house, his wife or mother came to the door and said he was busy, or indisposed.

Finally, James arranged an ambush with McLaughlin and hid behind the barn between the agent's house and office until Beckwith walked by. When he stepped out and shouted the agent's name, Beckwith snapped, "Not now, Doctor! I have urgent business with Mister McLaughlin."

"That's why I'm here. Mister McLaughlin asked me to tell you your meeting with him isn't necessary. His fears of trouble on the reservation appear to be unfounded. He's riding out now to make sure."

"Thank you, Doctor." Beckwith quickened his pace.

"Since you have the time now, I'll show you my health census results."

"Not now."

"It won't take long."

"Very well!"

James made his case with tables documenting large numbers of Indians suffering from scurvy, constipation, diarrhea and general lethargy from malnutrition.

"Far too many older people are falling ill and wasting away. The infant mortality rate is even more shocking, over fifty percent die between birth and age three. We've documented low birth weight, pneumonia and other ailments caused by poor nutrition."

"We're not here to feed the savages so they can continue their sinful polygamy and heathen dances," Beckwith declared. "We're not here to save their lives, Doctor. We're here to save their souls."

<hr />

"What's bothering you? I know that look," Fannie said as James chewed a bite of roast pork.

"I met with Beckwith today and explained our health census, didn't do any good. McLaughlin won't stick his neck out, either. I think the way he sees it, if Beckwith gets his way and cuts rations further, there will be an exodus or uprising and Beckwith will be fired. I don't stand a chance of getting rations increased as long as those two are fighting."

Fannie reached across the table. "You're doing the best you can."

"For all the good that does. Beckwith is despicable, but McLaughlin angers me more. He cares about his Indians, as he puts it, but puts his interests above theirs."

"I think he truly believes their suffering will lead to their salvation," Fannie replied, "but his words make me wince, too. Marie told me her husband says the Sioux are halter broke but not yet bitted, so they have to suffer more."

"Someone should tell him we don't starve our horses to train them for the bit."

"You could tell him."

6

Popping Trees Moon

In the dull round of life at the Devils Lake agency . . . nothing stands out so much as the frightful stress of the winter months, when isolated from the world, we were weather-bound for five or six months. . . . During the winter, there was nothing to be done but to house up and keep as comfortable as possible.
—"My Friend the Indian" by James McLaughlin

Fannie shivered behind the parlor window, thinking the mounted men outside looked more like escorts for a funeral procession than a recovery detail. Snow filled the brims of their dark hats and frosted their wool coats. Their burly, bearded scout, Tom Crayon, started his dogs and the fur-clad Indians ahead of him urged their ponies into the wind. James and the soldiers followed, and quickly disappeared like ghosts into the snowy veil.

Fannie turned away, checked the fire in the parlor stove and sat down with an unopened book in her lap. Tea time at the Hunts' quarters passed. She didn't want to hear the officers' wives' hollow, comforting words or their scolding disapproval of men determined to recover the soldier's body right away.

Restless, she tromped to the hospital, where she slipped quickly past Doctor Ferguson's office and pulled a chair up to Private John Mitzdorf's bed. The Seventh Cavalry soldier, terminally ill with syphilis, was sleeping. He looked so young—marble white skin with thin whiskers and short light brown hair. She wanted to hold him, comfort him like a child, give him the love she never had when she was a child.

When he woke up, she sponged his face and got him some soup. He managed a few spoonfuls and fell back asleep. She wiped a tear and slipped her arms into her coat draped over the back of the chair.

"Don't worry ma'am. Doctor DeWolf'll be fine," the matron said as she left.

◇ ◇ ◇

The thermometer outside the hospital read 15 below zero when she left. It must be colder now, she thought as everything faded to black outside.

Fear rose from the pit of her stomach and stuck in her throat. She knew Crayon's reputation. The legendary scout and mail carrier had survived every bad thing the northern plains could throw at a man, from ferocious blizzards and scorching heat to vagabonds and hostile Indians. Married to a mixed-blood fort servant, he knew the land and its people as well as any white man could.

Still, Fannie worried. He was only human.

She closed her eyes and drifted away, only to see James face-up on a snowy hill with his icy white face frozen in agony. A terrible scream pierced the wind's roar, a woman's scream. Her scream!

She wrapped her arms tightly over her chest and bent over and moaned. James was dead. She knew it. She went upstairs, got under the covers and lay wide awake for a long time. Finally, exhausted, she fell into a deep sleep, and emerged when she heard James's voice.

"Fannie?"

She put her hand on his thigh. He touched her forehead. "Are you ill?"

She clasped his hand. "When it got dark, and you didn't come back . . ."

"Finding that boy's body wasn't easy. He was buried under a drift. Only a bit of his hat brim and three fingertips were showing. No signs of foul play, he simply got lost and froze to death. By the time we loaded him on Crayon's dogsled, it was almost dark. We spent the night in a tepee at the braves' camp." He kissed Fannie's forehead. "I've got to go to the hospital for the autopsy."

She got up and dressed, and when she couldn't stand being alone any longer, went to the hospital, where she found James slumped over his desk with his head resting on the open medical log. "James?" He jerked up and rubbed his eyes.

"You're exhausted. You have a touch of frost bite on your cheeks."

"You're all right now?" he responded. She nodded. "The autopsy's finished, no surprises. The stewards dressed him in his best uniform and took his body to cold storage, where he'll stay until the ground's thawed enough for his burial."

James pushed the log across his desk and Fannie read his report:

Farris Mead, Co. L 7th Cavalry was sent out Saturday the 27th to a station about 17 miles distant from the post to examine and report on the condition of a government mule which had been injured and left there. Returning in the afternoon about 4 miles on their way home, the driver missed his whip and started back to find it. Mead got out and started walking back to the fort.

The team returned to the station before finding the whip and in coming home saw nothing of their companion. As a storm came up in the afternoon, it is assumed that Mead lost the road and wandered about until overcome by the cold. The body was found Dec. 1st by Indians about 2 or 3 miles distant from the spot where his comrades had last seen him. It is stated that he had a flask of whiskey in his possession though none was found with the body, and also that he had taken several drinks of whiskey while at the station. . . . The temperature on the 27th fell to 16 degrees during the night and continued to grow colder on the following day until the mercury reached minus 28 degrees, the mean temperature of the 28th being minus 22.26 degrees.

"Dying for the taste of whiskey, such a waste," she said. "If he'd only waited until he got back to the fort, he'd still be alive. He'd still have a chance to meet someone who loved him enough to ease his need for alcohol. The dance in two weeks, he might have met someone there."

"Fannie, you know that for many men there's no replacement for whiskey, not even a loving companion." A smile replaced his frown. "I am looking forward to the dance. I've heard the laundresses work up a pretty good lather and sometimes nearly bounce out of their low-cut dresses."

Fannie laughed. "I'll have to keep an eye on you."

"And I you," James replied. "Several officers have told me you're the prettiest lady to ever grace Fort Totten."

"Oh?" she asked in a teasing tone. "Who said that?"

"The bachelor officers, in particular Captain Abram Harbach. He had the audacity to say it's a good thing I found you before he did."

* * * * *

"Missus DeWolf, would you do me the honor?"

Fannie looked at James, who forced a smile, and she joined Captain Harbach on the dance floor as the fiddler struck up a lively version of *Turkey in the Straw*.

"Keep an eye on that man!" McDougall said. Fannie glanced back and thought she heard James reply, "You already told me."

The fiddler played a square dance version of *The Girl I Left Behind Me* and then announced he would slow things down with *Home Sweet Home* in waltz tempo. More couples left their tables. Harbach gripped Fannie's hand. "Will you dance the waltz?"

"I need a breather," Fannie replied, flushed and out of breath.

"I'd be honored." He smiled and bowed.

"Just one more then." She glanced at James who appeared to be smoldering. She flushed brighter red, aggravated that he wouldn't break in. He'd rather play the martyr. When the waltz ended, she pulled her hand away from Harbach's, looked directly at James, mouthed the words, "I love you," and quickly left the floor.

"James, dance with me please."

"I could never dance as well as you and Captain Harbach," he replied.

She pulled and he started to rise but was stopped by the sound of silver on glass.

"Attention everyone!" It was the post adjutant. "General Hunt has an important announcement."

The commanding officer rose and in a loud voice called, "Mister McDougall, please come forward." McDougall strode to the front of the room, where he stood at rigid attention. "Thomas Mower McDougall," the commanding officer announced in a loud, clear voice, "as of December fifteenth, eighteen seventy-five, you are appointed Captain, United States Army."

He presented McDougall his broad silver bars, and Alice was called up to pin them on.

"Missus Captain McDougall!" Fannie exclaimed as her friend returned.

James slapped his cavalry friend on the back, offering hearty congratulations, and then frowned as Captain Harbach approached their table again. "Missus DeWolf?"

She shook her head and took James's hand, but he smiled and said, "Go ahead."

○ ● ○ ○

Fannie held James's arm tightly on the way back to their quarters. Northern lights shimmered in the star-studded sky. "Have you ever seen anything more beautiful?"

"You," James replied. "Dancing tonight, you were the loveliest woman in the world. You're so beautiful, Fannie. It's no wonder Captain Harbach is drawn to you."

"Oh, James." She squeezed his arm, thinking maybe now he'd learn to dance.

James added wood to the coals in the parlor stove. Fannie reached for him when he stood. "Don't fret. You know I love only you."

"I feel all men see you as I do, adore you, want you."

She laughed and then said seriously, "I adore you, James. I'm so proud of everything you've done, and I cherish everything we've done together, in Oregon, Boston, and now here at the fort and in the Indian camps." She put her arms around him and kissed him. "I thank God every morning when I wake up by your side."

"I know I'm foolish, but Captain Harbach pays far too much attention to you."

She looked into his eyes. "If his intentions are anything but honorable, he'll suffer the wounds of great disappointment."

James knew he should stop. "To others, it might appear you encourage his flirtations."

"Is that how it appears to you?" Fannie flared. And then more calmly: "We can't stop people from talking."

***

The week before Christmas, Fannie was in the kitchen slicing bread and cutting ham for their mid-day meal when she heard James stomp into the entry and slam the front door. One boot crashed against the entry wall and then the other. She hurried out of the kitchen and found James in his stocking feet with his fists clenched.

"What's wrong?"

"Do you know what it's like, being lectured when everyone can hear?"

"What are you talking about?"

"Ernst Brenner! He scolded me for your reckless spending!"

She flushed. "Is that what he said? How dare he!"

"He lectured me," he repeated, "about your irresponsible . . ."

"How dare you take his side!"

"And said monetary indiscretions could ruin my career."

"What career?"

"Came right into the surgeons' office, and in front of Doctor Ferguson told me he had private matters to discuss. It was humiliating!"

"Welcome to the club!"

"Doctor Ferguson scurried out to the ward," James said, "but he and everybody heard, or at least knew why Brenner was there." He pulled off his wool scarf and coat and threw them at a chair.

Fannie flushed. "Now you know how I was made to feel!"

"You do the purchasing, not me!"

"So it's all right for him to bully me but not you, is that what you're saying?"

"I trust you to buy what we need, and manage our finances. Maybe I shouldn't."

"Well then, you buy everything! You have no idea how much everything costs here, do you, or how much those land payments to your brother affect our budget."

James took a deep breath and lowered his voice. "Maybe I should pay more attention, but Mister Brenner said you're putting too much on account, for canned fruit, eggs, flour and sugar, and for soaps and toiletries."

"Brenner's just angry because I don't let him push me around. Washing with soap, brushing your teeth with powder, is too much? James, he bullies everyone that way, no matter what they buy. And everyone at the fort knows it."

In a more subdued tone, James said, "I promised him I would talk to you."

"What we buy and how we pay for it is our affair!"

"We are indebted to him, Fannie, he has a say. We could cut back on some things, couldn't we? You know we have another farm payment due. My mother has complained about our overdue loan."

"She's well aware of our temporary financial difficulties. You've told her in your letters about our travel expenses and the high prices out here. Maybe we should just forget the farm, as you suggested, let your brother and parents take your share. We could move back to

Boston, where you could join the Massachusetts General staff."

"Or stay in the Army," James said under his breath.

"What?"

"Nothing."

"You're not staying in the Army, if that's what you said."

○ ◦ ▨ ◦ ▨ ◦

Three days later, two cavalry privates left the fort on foot to buy whiskey at a ranch about seven miles away. Their bodies were found the next day. James wrote in the log that the low temperature was 20 degrees the night they died, and *although frozen, there can be no doubt whatever that had they been sober these men would have returned to their quarters in perfect safety.*

"I can't stop thinking about those poor men," Fannie said to James as they dressed for Christmas dinner at the Hunts' quarters. "It's a sin what liquor does to men."

James smiled. "There'll be plenty of excess today."

She took her cherished necklace from her jewelry box. Rubies around the gold cross glittered. She turned it over and read her initials, *F.D.* "It's so beautiful, James. Would you fasten it for me?"

He secured the clasp and pressed close, then broke away and opened his pocket watch. "We'd better go." He headed downstairs, leaving Fannie to fuss with her hair. "Fannie!" he shouted a few minutes later.

"I'm coming!" She found him pacing. "I'll get the cake, your favorite, devil's food with white frosting coated with dark chocolate, even though the ingredients cost too much."

"Just get it! It's time to go!"

She carefully placed the cake in a decorated box, took it out to the parlor, set it on an end table and put on her coat with no rush. On their way to the Hunts', James said, "You could have had the cake ready last night."

She held her tongue. At the Hunts', he sighed when he saw that most of the guests were already there. A servant girl took the cake, another took their coats. "I love your dress," General Hunt's wife told

Fannie. "The tailoring is exquisite and the fine gray wool becomes you. Did you buy it in Boston?"

"I bought the fabric and lace there. I made the dress."

Captain Harbach looked directly into Fannie's eyes and surveyed her figure. "It is a beautiful dress and lovely necklace, too."

"Thank you, Captain," she answered formally. "The necklace is my wedding gift from my husband." She took James's hand and squeezed.

Edna Ferguson came downstairs with her baby, Jimmie, on her shoulder, and the Hunts led everyone into the dining room. General Hunt thanked the Lord for their blessings, and they dug into a feast of roast pork and chicken, mashed potatoes, corn and candied yams with water and wine. After dessert, the men went to the parlor to sample General Hunt's brandy while the women sipped tea in the kitchen.

Later, Fannie joined James by a front window. Strains of a fiddle, shouts and laughter drifted across the parade ground from the barracks. The snow sparkled like refined sugar in the sun.

"At times like this, winter seems more magical than daunting," Fannie said.

"Merry Christmas Fannie."

"Merry Christmas James."

<hr />

As bad as January was, February was worse. Wind roared between the fort's white brick buildings, reducing visibility to zero and piling drifts above the second-story eaves in some places. Cavalrymen slept in shifts in the stables to care for the horses. Laundresses and servants slept in the laundry building next to the barracks, so they wouldn't have to walk between their shacks and the fort. Each night, a few more women slipped into the barracks, where they shared liquor, levity and carnal pleasures with the men. One cold, starry night, their activities blossomed into a raucous party that went on for hours before the duty officer finally trudged through the deep snow and broke it up.

General Hunt issued an order the next day: *The verbal permission granted laundryes to burn lights after taps having been abused, it is hereby withdrawn. . . . No dances will be permitted in Company Quarters at any hours for both sexes without permission from the Commanding Officer.*

• ⬤ •

Fannie missed visiting Wenonah, Walks Behind and the other Dakota women she had come to know. She worried about Walks Behind's son, Caske, too.

The boy was light as a bird the last time she cradled him in her arms. She'd taken pureed meat and carrots, had fed him and left what remained, about a week's supply. That was over three weeks ago, but the brutal weather made it impossible to return.

So Fannie spent more time at Mitzdorf's bedside. The young soldier was so afraid and lonesome. She could see it in his pale gray eyes. He didn't talk much. He was shy and didn't speak very good English, but it was clear he was attached to her. She could see that in his eyes, too.

She spooned cool water and warm broth into his dry, sore mouth. She applied ointment to his lips and sores. She wanted to do everything for him, but when it came to cleaning and caring for his most private areas, he insisted that the matron perform the duties, not her.

When she wasn't feeding and caring for him, she held his hand, stroked his hair and read to him from the Bible. She didn't know how much he understood, but it was clear her readings and company meant everything to him.

"He's suffering terribly," she told James one day. "The matron says the urethral suppositories are incredibly painful, and I can see that the mercury pills' side effects—the tremors and nausea—are much worse than any good they might be doing."

James discontinued the suppositories and pills and increased Mitzdorf's opium.

On March 6, 1876, John Mitzdorf, Pvt., Company E Seventh

Cavalry, was discharged from the Army. James told Doctor Ferguson they had no choice but to keep him in the hospital. Ferguson notified General Hunt that Mitzdorf was *unable in his present condition to leave the hospital. . . . I would therefore respectfully ask that he be allowed to remain in Hospital and that a ration be issued to him from the Post Commissary.*

The request was granted.

7

March 10, 1876 - This morning, Companies "E" and "L" 7th Cavalry left this post for Fort Seward en route to Fort Abraham Lincoln D.T. where they are to form part of the force under General Custer— with which it is intended to operate against Indians. Capt. McDougall, Lt. Craycroft and Act. Asst. Surgeon DeWolf U.S.A. accompanied this squadron.

—Fort Totten Medical History log

James paused in the doorway to the hospital ward and watched Fannie patiently spoon broth into Private Mitzdorf's mouth. She wiped his chin, waited, and spooned again. Each sip was painful for the soldier because of his sores, but he needed the nourishment. She set the bowl aside and held Mitzdorf's hand.

How could he ever be jealous of her? He felt for Mitzdorf, perhaps as much as she did, but the private drew his comfort from her. She was Mitzdorf's angel, and his angel, too. He walked up behind her and put a hand on her shoulder.

"What's wrong?" she asked, reading his face.

"Let's go to our quarters." Outside, he told her. "The new cavalry officer from Louisiana arrived, with orders. Our companies are moving to Fort Lincoln, where they'll join the rest of the Seventh for an expedition to the Yellowstone. We leave in two days."

Fannie kept her eyes on the slippery boardwalk. "You mean a campaign, don't you, against the Indians."

She looked into his eyes and he nodded: "They had until the end of January to return to their reservations. Tom McDougall says Generals Sherman and Sheridan want to punish the bands that refused to heed the order."

"Going after them now, in this weather? Didn't it occur to them that maybe that's why the Indians are still out there?"

James sighed. "There's nothing I can do."

She fussed around the kitchen after supper, making more noise than usual. James poked the parlor stove fire and added a log. He couldn't think. "I'm going for a walk." She didn't answer, but he knew from the pause in her activity that she'd heard him.

Orange halos glowed in icy fog around the boardwalk's lanterns. The damp cold knifed through his coat. No one else was out. Circling the parade ground, he tried to get a grip on his thoughts and feelings. In over four years of marriage, he and Fannie had never been apart.

Around and around he went, circling and circling, always ending where he started. He didn't want to leave Fannie, didn't want to share her with his family in Pennsylvania, didn't want to move back to Boston, didn't want to risk losing her from childbirth.

Around and around, back to where he began. He didn't want to leave.

He went back inside. Fannie had put out the lamps and candles, so it was pitch dark. He tiptoed upstairs, where he found her sound asleep. He undressed and slipped in beside her, put a hand on her waist and felt her soft breathing.

"I'll be in the barracks all afternoon," he said during dinner the next day, "inspecting the cavalry companies for cold-weather readiness."

She crossed her arms tightly. "I had tea at Missus Hunt's this morning. The ladies say it's crazy, leaving this time of year. Missus Fletcher says I should make you a hood. Maybe you should buy more long underwear, too."

"We don't have the money," James replied. "I have to go."

He was still studying his Seventh Cavalry soldiers' medical records when Fannie walked by on her way to the ward. A few minutes later, she came into the office.

"Mitzdorf is asleep. I'm going back to our quarters."

"Your wife looks tired. She's taking it hard?" Ferguson asked after she left.

"She is," James responded. "It's hard for me, too, but I'll be busy, moving to Lincoln and then preparing for the expedition. She'll be here waiting and worrying. I'm afraid she might succumb to melancholia. I've seen what it can do. A soldier in Oregon nearly died of it after his sweetheart succumbed to pneumonia. He didn't want to get out of bed, wouldn't eat or drink much, or even speak. I was the hospital steward who delivered his empty shell to an insane asylum in San Francisco."

"I've seen it, too," Ferguson said. "It's not that uncommon during our long Dakota winters. But don't worry, Missus Ferguson and I will keep an eye on your wife."

◆ ◆ ◆

Fannie threw her arms around him and kissed him passionately when he returned to their quarters that evening. He broke her clutch and searched her face. "Fannie." His eyes moistened and voice cracked. "You look wonderful."

"I made chicken and dumplings and peach pie for desert." She embraced him again and whispered, "I'm all right. Don't worry."

She cleared the table after their meal while he sipped brandy in the parlor. When she joined him, he thought she'd never looked more beautiful, not even on their wedding day when she beamed with love, standing before the chaplain.

She took his hand and led him upstairs. They embraced and

kissed with bruising force, tearing at each other's clothing, then melded in rapture so intense it was as if they'd ascended to heaven.

Fannie panted in the afterglow. He rolled over onto his back, expecting she would get up. Instead, she kissed him, mussed his hair and tenderly lipped his forehead, then the outline of his face from his temples to his chin. She found his lips again through his mustache.

"Fannie, shouldn't you?"

"Hold me."

"Fannie!"

She sighed, got up, put on her robe and slippers and walked to the smaller bedroom, where they kept their chamber pot and she her personal items. She removed what she needed from a small trunk, prepared the mixture and filled the syringe. She looked at it—hesitated—and then emptied its contents into the chamber pot, put everything away and slipped back into bed.

"I love you, Fannie."

"I love *you*."

He took a deep breath. "There's something I must tell you before I leave. I want to stay another year. I believe we both would enjoy a warm season here."

"James . . ."

"Please, hear me out. I haven't finished what I've started, what we've started here with the Indians. I've, we've, barely begun."

"Let's not talk about it tonight. There will be time when you return."

They fell asleep in each others' arms.

Seemingly moments later, in the pre-dawn dark, James heard loud pounding and a call for him to rise. The next thing he noticed was the roar of the wind.

◆ ◆ ◆

Left Totten at 9 AM 10 degrees below zero.
—Doctor J.M. DeWolf diary entry, March 10th 1876

His eyes found her huddled with the other women in front of

the stables. Frozen tears streaked her wind-burned cheeks. He felt a pang of sadness and regret.

General Hunt and the other fort officers leaned into the blizzard with the women, waiting for Companies E and L to pass in review. McDougall gave the command and the big cavalry horses shuffled up the hill from the frozen lake, snorting plumes of fog. James looked into Fannie's eyes and touched his hat with three fingers, meaning, one-two-three, "I love you." She placed three fingers on her lips, waved and mouthed the words. He smiled. "Don't worry," his lips said.

At the top of a low rise near a towering drift, he looked back one last time but Fannie was gone. He felt heartsick for a moment and then realized his big, bay gelding was chomping at the bit. He yanked on the reins as his horse lurched into Crayon's.

"Stay back, Doctor!" the burly scout yelled over his shoulder.

His horse charged again and dug its teeth into the haunches of Crayon's paint. The scout's spirited pony reared, and Crayon yelled angrily, "Control your mount!" James jerked the reins hard, but the big horse strained ahead, chomping at the haunches of Crayon's pony. The scout wheeled his horse and moved next to James. "Control your damn horse, Doctor!"

James jerked his reins savagely. The horse reared; his hind quarters slipped out from under him, and he crashed hard, catching James's left leg and foot under the full force of his weight. James screamed in pain but held the reins as the terrified animal bellowed, thrashed and scrambled in the snow, dragging James with him.

Crayon leaped from his paint and handed his horse's reins to McDougall. He grabbed the reins of James's horse and angrily pulled the thrashing animal to its feet. Holding tightly just under the bit, he jerked the horse's head down. "Are you all right, Doctor!?"

"My foot! I believe it's broken!" James tried to stand and fell when he put weight on the injured foot.

Crayon helped James up. "You have to get back on!"

Gritting his teeth, he grabbed the saddle and pulled himself up. Light-headed, he lowered his head momentarily to keep from falling.

"Ride up front with us!" Crayon yelled.

James moved his horse between McDougall's and Crayon's. The big gelding's nostrils flared; he fought the bit briefly, then settled down, content as long as there was no horse in front of him.

"How's your foot?" McDougall asked.

"Hurts like hell!"

"We'll find you a different mount tomorrow!"

"This horse and I have come to an understanding! I'll keep him!"

After several brutal hours, the column turned south, putting the wind at the riders' backs. "There's an abandoned ranch near the Sheyenne River," McDougall said. "We'll camp there."

"Any buildings?" James asked.

"Nope, just some hills north of a fallen-down sod house," McDougall replied.

○ ○ ○

Four months of snow and wind had sculpted a long, high drift with an overhang along the undulating hills. They pitched their tents under its shelter, with the howling wind carrying a white ceiling of snow above them.

"Three wagons still out!" a sergeant reported to McDougall. "One's broken down. They're transferring everything into the other two!"

They started fires with wood gathered from trees hugging the hills. James sat by one and examined each man for frostbite. It was long past dark when he finished. The men who came in late with the stranded wagons were worst off.

"One of the teamsters has frozen fingertips. Three soldiers have frozen feet and one frozen fingers. Just about every soldier's hands and feet are chilled," James told McDougall.

7 AM Broke camp, the wind blowing furiously. The guide after going about one mile could not find the road, went on 3 miles and the wind increased & continued snowing so objects were invisible at a very short distance. Turned back and with great difficulty followed our trail back to

old camp. Numerous were the frosted noses & faces but none very severely frosted, my face slightly. My foot is painful but not disabled.
　　　　　　　　　　　　　　　—DeWolf diary entry March 11, 1876

They huddled under the drift all of the second day. James tried to take his mind off the painful cold with warm thoughts of Fannie—touching her in bed, listening to her soft, even breathing as she slept, her beautiful eyes and smile, her succulent lips when they kissed. He wished he'd let her make him a hood. He wished he hadn't made an issue about no money for long underwear.

Shortly before dark, the snow tapered off. The stinging wind was unrelenting, but they managed to gather wood. The fires saved them that night, when the temperature fell to 20 below.

The third day dawned clear and calm, offering relief as they crossed the frozen Sheyenne River. The snowy plains rolled endlessly around them and gave off an almost unbearable glare by mid-morning. James's horse led the way with Crayon's, slipping over icy crests and plowing through deep drifts in the hollows.

Just before noon, a scout and two soldiers arrived from Fort Seward with a telegram for McDougall, who read the dispatch and jammed it into his coat pocket. "Devil be damned! They send us off to near-certain death and then tell us the expedition might be delayed until the weather improves!" He rode a short distance with his back to the men, drank a stiff jolt from his flask and quickly put it away, wiping his lips. "That's the damned Army!"

Another storm hit that third night, waking James, McDougall and William Craycroft in the white canvas wall tent they shared.

"If we don't make Fort Seward tomorrow, we'll freeze to death," McDougall said.

Snow packed into their mustaches and beards, melted next to their skin and refroze, burning like fire. They followed traces of the trail from windswept hilltop to windswept hilltop. The wind calmed, the snow stopped and the skies cleared shortly after noon.

At mid-afternoon, a second detail from Seward arrived with another telegram. It evoked more cursing from McDougall, for it informed him that Companies E and L could delay their trip to Fort Lincoln, at their discretion, until the weather was safe for travel.

The sun set and they pushed on toward Fort Seward, following the trail by moonlight.

8

Snowblind Moon

Major Rodway Smith, paymaster USA arrived this afternoon and reported having met the Cavalry a few miles this side of the [S]heyenne where they stopped to join camp. . . . Several of the men were frostbitten, to what extent is not known but the day has been very cold owing to a strong Northwest wind and the thermometer below zero.
—March 10, 1876 entry in Fort Totten Medical History log

Another howling blizzard raged outside, the third in the seven days since James departed. Not a wagon, horse or dogsled had traveled the eighty-two miles between forts Totten and Seward since she'd received his first letters, all written on the trail. The one she needed, the letter telling her he was safe and sound at Fort Seward, still hadn't come.

The blinding snow blew for two more excruciating days and nights, and then the sun rose gloriously, gilding the snowy hills. It wouldn't be long now, Fannie thought, before mail from Seward arrived at Totten. Would the sled bring letters from James, or a notice of his death? There was no way to know.

She helped Edna with her domestic duties and spent hours working at the hospital in a futile effort to keep her mind off her worst fears. She was sponging Mitzdorf's face when the calls finally came on March 21. "Carrier! Carrier from Seward!" Rushing to a window, she watched and waited until she couldn't stand it anymore. She went back to Mitzdorf and clutched the soldier's hand.

"Letters for Missus DeWolf!" She ran to the entry hall, grabbed them and hurried to their quarters.

Such a trip is like placing one on the brink of a precipice and giving him a push. . . . Now I think I can stand as much as any human being.

In the next letter:

Darling wife,

You cannot imagine how much I feel our separation this time and hope it will not be necessary again. Everything is like a dream to me. I do not like rooming with tobacco consumers. Such a room as we keep you ought to see, three guns in one corner, one in another, two pistols hung on the wall. Our dressing table . . . has everything you can think of on it in confusion. The window is full of cartridge shells, powder, flask, hammer, gloves, wristlets. . . . Every corner is full of old boots. . . . The walls are adorned with hats, caps, bridle, stirrups, riding whips, guitar, boots, smoking pouches, pants, overcoats. . . . The quarters are some like the rooms at Totten. We occupy the . . . dining room. . . . The front room has a table & stove & a lot of truck & is the passage way to our paradise, though we are happy. . . . Love & kisses darling, from your loving Husb J.M. DeWolf

She finished the letters, bowed her head, closed her eyes and whispered, "He's alive."

More storms slashed across the plains, but their frequency diminished, allowing mail delivery once, sometimes twice, a week. Fannie lived for his letters, and warmed when she read that he lived for hers, too.

I have just read your splendid letters. They find me with a headache today but only from Seidletz Powders [a mild laxative]. . . . The wind is commencing to blow. . . . I am sick of writing about the road being open. . . . I am so glad you are having such good times.

She enjoyed his descriptions of his four roommates. Doctor DuBray, a Seward surgeon, smoked his pipe, read magazines and newspapers and pontificated on everything from the progress of civilization and how it affected the Indians to corruption in Washington and Brevet General George Armstrong Custer's chances of becoming president. *He is an Englishman and is like all of his countrymen, English.* Captain Maize, an infantry officer, smoked, drank, cleaned his guns, polished his boots and said very little. *I admire Capt. McDougall the more I know him*, even though he smokes and drinks as much as the others. Craycroft *I cannot say I do*, for he's a blowhard full of high-flown phrases.

She wrote that she was doing her best to keep busy so their time apart would pass more quickly. She spent considerable time each day at the hospital, tending to Mitzdorf and other sick soldiers, but the snow was still too deep for travel to the reservation. She enjoyed tea, needlework and knitting with the other officers' wives. She helped Edna Ferguson with Jimmie and with meals since she was eating dinners and suppers with the Fergusons now. She was taking piano lessons from the commanding officer's wife and played lively duets with her to the delight of the other ladies. She and Alice McDougall were especially close, since their husbands were both in the Seventh Cavalry. Alice was steadfast in her conviction that their husbands would return safe and sound.

James wrote back:

Tell Mrs. Hunt, Mrs. Fletcher & Mrs. Ferguson & Dr. that I am very grateful for their kindness to you and Mrs. McDougall that I admire her bravery. . . . Hoping you are well and happy. I once more assure you that my anxiety & troubles are all and solely for you my darling wife. . . . Your loving husband, love & kisses,

J.M. DeWolf

My letters I think contain all that would interest you. . . . We have beer but I only drink one glass a day & no whiskey since the first day. . . . Don't fear my drinking for you have no reason.

Fannie smiled when she read about his moderate alcohol consumption, and smiled again when she read that he might buy collars from a merchant in nearby Jamestown at half the fort trader's price, even though it was against regulations. He hoped to send her enough money to settle their account with Brenner, *but do not mention this to others or about the price* of the collars.

Her spirits sank when his next letters were delivered by McDougall. He'd been ordered to Shreveport, where he would take command of Company B, and was picking up Alice so they could travel together to Fort Seward, where they would stay for awhile before continuing to Louisiana.

Seeing her friend beaming with happiness, knowing she and her husband would be together, broke her heart. Why not James? Why couldn't *they* be going to Shreveport, too? Then life would be wonderful again.

James was heartsick, too. She could tell, for he told her that in case she was entirely sick of Totten, *you must not feel that you are compelled to remain there for I will let you go home. . . . Hoping you are happy & content as your happiness is my happiness.*

Pen in hand, she was determined to open her heart, to tell James everything—how much she loved him, how he meant everything to her, how and why she deceived him the night before he left.

She tried to find the right words. He was leaving on a dangerous campaign. She might never see him again. Over and over, she tried to frame her thoughts and feelings in a way he'd understand. Again and again, she threw her wadded efforts into the parlor stove. She'd wait until she knew for sure she was pregnant.

"I miss you more than ever and wish you were here," she wrote. "I promise I will continue my piano lessons. They are most enjoyable and I know they are good for me. Captain Harbach asked me to join him on the floor, but I declined. Please give my regards to the McDougalls."

His next letter said he'd received a letter from his parents. They wanted a second note for his medical school debt: *I am a mind to tell them something. If I was sure of my money I would not sign it.* Fannie flushed when she read the next part, for it was a lecture about how she should conduct herself in his absence, *particularly you should fasten your doors at night, if not for safety, for fashion. . . . Darling, I hope I do not annoy you by the advice above for mother's letter annoys me.*

Love and kisses from your loving husband, J.M. DeWolf

"Your worries regarding my safety and 'fashion' are for naught, darling," she replied. "I assure you I am always alone and have no reason to lock my doors. It's nice you are concerned for my welfare, as I am for yours."

A week later he wrote about playing whist with officers and ladies and hearing a young woman at the next card table *remark that she liked Capt. Harbach very much.*

In a postscript, he added: *I think darling you had better if you can get some one to sleep in the house with you at nights, as you will not feel like being alone many nights. You may be able to get Stewarts' daughter or some one else. From your loving husband J.M.D.*

Her reply was more pointed this time: "You needn't worry about whether I have a female companion sleeping with me at night. You needn't worry about my doors being locked, either, for safety or appearances. I believe I already told you that. Again, I assure you James, I am always alone, and thinking only of you.

"Your Loving Wife, F.J.D.

"P.S. Can't you take leave and come see me?"

He'd like to come see her, he replied, but he had only one week's leave. *I would be near all of that time on the road going & returning.* Besides, the expedition might be abandoned, *but do not hope so too much. Darling, it seems hard that we must be separated but perhaps it will come all right in time . . . love & kisses to my darling wife*

A week's leave, Fannie thought, even if he spent four days coming and going, would give them four glorious nights and three days. She could tell him everything. She wiped her eyes and started a letter, pleading for him to take the leave and come see her. But she knew James. He wouldn't change his mind. She crumpled the paper.

9

I think you will get no less than three or four letters from me this mail & one I think I forgot to seal thinking I might want to put in a few more words. The telegraph operator is off drunk. I should think he would get crazy as all the officers go down & buzz him 'til he cannot attend to his business or anything else. They play with his apparatus & really run him.

—Letter from James to Fannie

James rested a hand on the private's shoulder. "I'll have to take three or four."

"I seen 'em Doc, figgered as much. Better toes than a foot or leg. It'll be my ticket home, or maybe to them Black Hills gold fields."

"You may have a feeling of suffocation from the chloroform. It'll pass quickly."

The steward placed a cone over the soldier's mouth and nose and poured a measured dose of chloroform onto a cloth inside. The soldier's eyes darted in panic. He struggled violently, and then relaxed. James touched an eyelid, which contracted reflexively. "A little more chloroform." He waited, touched an eyelid again, and then slapped the soldier sharply. "Can you hear me, private?"

The soldier, draped from chin to ankles in the Fort Seward Hospital operating room, didn't respond. James worked quickly, making a circular cut through skin and flesh at the base of the large toe of the right foot. A steward kept the skin pulled back, and James cut through the bone with a small finger saw. The toe dropped into a bucket.

James repeated the procedure on the second toe. The hospital matron wiped the bloody stubs with swabs soaked in laudanum and dressed the wounds. James started with the knife on the soldier's left foot, removing the big toe and the one next to it. He wanted the toes off and the wounds dressed before the young man started coming around.

"When he wakes up, keep him on just enough morphine to manage the pain."

The day was March 29, the day Custer testified before a House committee about War Department corruption. It was also the day First Lieutenants James Calhoun and Algernon Smith arrived at Seward to take command of the two Totten companies. They were waiting for James when he exited the surgery room.

James beamed at the sight of his old friend Calhoun, a tall man with sandy hair and mustache and an infectious, confident smile. "Mister Calhoun." He extended his hand. "And you must be Captain Algernon Smith," he added, acknowledging the light-haired, fresh-faced man with Calhoun.

"Brevet Captain," the soft-spoken Smith said.

"Congratulations on your new commands." James felt his spirits lift. It wasn't just the reunion with his old friend from Camp Warner. The men brought a fresh feeling of optimism. McDougall was entertaining, but his wit had a wearing, cynical edge, and he turned moody when he drank too much.

"It's been awhile," James said to Calhoun.

Calhoun nodded. "When did you get your medical degree?"

"Last June. Missus DeWolf and I met and married at Warner after you left," James replied. "And I hear you married Custer's sister."

"Just over three years ago."

They rode into Jamestown and stopped at a saloon.

"I enjoy a beer or a shot of whiskey now and then, but I couldn't keep up with McDougall and the others at Totten," James said after sipping from his beer mug.

"McDougall's a good man, but he's his own worst enemy," Calhoun replied, "got court-martialed while stationed down South, you know, for drunk and disorderly."

"No, I didn't know."

"Yup, he was acquitted, but he's most definitely in Custer's doghouse."

"Tell me about Custer, what can I expect on the expedition?" James asked.

Smith smiled. "Custer does everything with flair. He had the band strike up *Garry Owen* in the middle of our fight with Sitting Bull on the Yellowstone in seventy-three."

"I learned that song drinking with McDougall and the others at Totten, still had the melody in my head the next morning, along with a terrible hangover. Think we'll have a fight this year?"

"Nah, not likely," Calhoun replied. "I think the fight's pretty much out of 'em."

A woman in a low-cut dress stopped by their table.

"One more? I'm buying," James said. "And tell me more about Custer."

"He doesn't drink, but he plays poker with the best," Smith said. "Everybody still talks about an all-night game at Fort Riley, Kansas, in the winter of sixty-seven. I joined the Seventh in August that year, and that game was one of the first things I heard about. Custer won early, but then Captain Benteen started winning. By dawn, he'd cleaned everybody out."

They all laughed, and then Smith turned serious. "There's bad blood between Custer and Benteen."

They stopped at the post office, where James found several letters from Fannie. At the telegraph office, the operator handed Calhoun a press dispatch. "Custer's being reassigned to the Rio Grande," Calhoun said with a frown. "General Terry's leading the expedition."

"Rumors go around and around here," James responded. "That one made the rounds a couple days ago, the story going that the Republicans wanted to send Custer to Texas so he wouldn't have a glorious victory over the Sioux that could pave his way to the White House. Another version had him missing the expedition because the Democrats want to keep him in Washington for more War Department corruption testimony."

A few days later, James rode into town with McDougall to check for news. The telegraph office was locked, so they rode to the Buffalo Bones Saloon, where James ordered beer and McDougall a bottle and a shot glass.

"I imagine you've met the officers taking command of our Totten companies."

"Had a beer with 'em a couple days ago."

"They're both Custer favorites, you know," McDougall said to James, downing a shot and pouring another. "Calhoun's married to Custer's sister, as I'm sure you know, and Smith's an ass kisser. Meanwhile, I'm being banished to the South again and probably left out of yet another expedition, my third missed in a row."

"Why would Custer single you out?" James asked.

"You'd have to ask him."

"You were promoted to captain, with his recommendation."

"I'll never make major." McDougall downed another shot. "How do you do it?"

"Do what?" James looked surprised.

"Control your drinking. I know you caught hell that first night at Totten, that's how it goes. And you didn't drink any more whiskey until our first night down here, did you?"

"Fannie told me she wouldn't tolerate a drunkard. She meant it." James's eyes misted. "I couldn't bear losing her."

"Alice threatened to move back to South Carolina if I didn't shape up. I couldn't stand losing her, either, but the whiskey has a grip. I've told myself over and over, no liquor today, can't do it."

James stared absently at the young woman at the bar, thinking of Fannie. He knew more than a few men who'd give up everything and everyone they loved for a bottle of whisky. He might have, too, before he met Fannie. He looked away when he realized the barmaid was smiling at him. She came to their table and leaned over, revealing deep cleavage. "Would you like another beer, and buy me one, too?"

McDougall smiled. James hesitated and then nodded. She returned with two beers, sat down beside him and leaned close, pressing her breasts against his arm and stirring his passions. He gulped down the last of his first beer and started the second. He was half finished with it when she asked him if he'd like to go upstairs. He flushed. McDougall grinned. "Go ahead, Doc, what's the harm? Everybody gets lonely."

She pressed closer, pulled him up and led him upstairs to a room, where she kissed him, encouraged him with her hand and pulled him onto the bed.

"I'm sorry." He pushed her off and rushed out the door. Still flushed and flustered, he hurried past McDougall, out of the tavern.

He poured his heart out that night and the next day:

Darling, do you get along pleasantly? I really hope you do and hope to send you some funds as soon as I can put in my pay acts for April. . . . I am so sorry you are so lonely up there. I am as much mortified as you at this damned fool move this spring but cannot help it. . . . I stay some days nearly all day in my quarters. . . . I should be most happy to chat with you if only for an hour but 80 miles of snow and slush divides us. . . . I am lonesome without you and it seems hard to be separated but darling I am doing as well as you could wish morally

Bye darling from your ever true & loving husband

<hr />

Heavy, wet snow fell and then it melted to mud under a warm April sun. Ducks and geese streamed north, resting on lakes and ponds around Fort Seward. Doctor DuBray bagged six ducks, *so we expect to have ducks for dinner tomorrow,* James wrote Fannie. *Won't they be good. I wish we could have dinner together.*

The day after the duck feast, he rode into town for a beer with his roommates, making sure they didn't stop at the Buffalo Bones, where the young lady worked. Taking a table in the middle of the room, McDougall and the others asked for a bottle and shot glasses. James ordered beer and was half finished when Ernst Brenner walked in.

"Brenner!" James waved at the Fort Totten trader.

McDougall glanced up distastefully and resumed his conversation with DuBray.

"Would you join us? What brings you to Jamestown?" James asked.

McDougall downed a shot, looked at James and said, "No offense to you, Doc, but he's not welcome."

Brenner flushed. "When you have time, Doctor DeWolf, we do have business."

"Excuse me," James said. He and Brenner went to a table near the front window.

"It's the matter of your account. In your absence, your wife has been somewhat imprudent in her purchases."

"What purchases?"

"Some yarn, dress fabric, buttons and thread. She'll require essentials while you're gone, but no more frivolities. You must deal with your account, and while it's not my place to say, with your wife."

"I'm afraid I can't settle now," James said. "The expedition is expected to be out until August, perhaps September. By then, I'll have several months' pay. I assure you I can settle in full when I return."

"It creates some difficulty for me. Your account is considerable, and there are others who owe, of course."

"If you can wait until I return," James said.

"I leave for Fort Totten in two days. I suggest you look for a way to pay at least part of your account," Brenner said. "You must tell your wife, only the absolute necessaries while you're away."

"I will, I assure you," James said.

"There's another matter. Missus DeWolf has made intemperate comments regarding matters that don't concern her," Brenner said.

"What matters?" James asked.

"Matters having to do with the management of the Indian agency and my store, personal things about me and Mister Beckwith that come back to me from others. It would be better for you and your wife if she would be more discreet."

"I'm sure she doesn't mean to offend, but I'll let her know. I have to go." James knocked over his chair in his hurry to leave.

That evening, he thought about his meeting with Brenner but was too angry and upset to write about it. Instead, he told Fannie: *I hope it will not be so dreary after spring comes and it will not be long before we have nice weather.*

He vented some of his anger by telling her that he intended to stay at Fort Totten for at least another year, *so you may not tell Mrs H. that I don't want to.* He'd sent his March pay, $125, to his brother Erastus for the farmland. He would get his April pay as soon as he could and send her fifty dollars. *You must keep your mess bill current,* he wrote.

Give my kindest regards to Mrs Hunt, Mrs Fletcher, Mrs Ferguson & the Baby. . . . I have been dreaming of you for several nights. . . . Well bye bye darling, Love and kisses from your loving Husband J M DeWolf

Fannie replied that her mess bill was current but she had no choice but to put necessities on their account with Brenner.

"I wish you were here. It's so lonely without you, especially alone in our quarters. Music lifts my spirits more than you could know. Playing duets with General Hunt's wife is a joy. I always sit with her and Edna during the Saturday night dances. The banjos and fiddles are delightful, and it is so much fun watching the ladies and men kick up their heels. Captain Harbach no longer asks me to dance. I've made it clear to him and to everyone that I will not dance while you are away. I help with Jimmie and spend several hours a day with Private Mitzdorf. His woes are infinitely worse than ours, yet he never complains."

She told him just about everyone at Totten had fallen ill with influenza. It ran through the barracks and servants' shacks, and then through the hospital and down officers' row. She suffered a high fever for a day and a night and was bedridden for two days.

"I'm fine now, so you needn't worry about me. General Hunt has suffered more than most and is still bedridden. I miss you so much, my dear. Please give my regards to Alice McDougall and remind her how much I admire her cheerful spirit and bravery."

He wrote in his reply that he was glad she was feeling better.

I have had one glass of beer this week and have gained two pounds, 177. I shall send you some funds from Lincoln. The news about Custer's assignment to the Rio Grande was a hoax, *and I was only one of several victims.*

He started his next letter with small talk: He'd received a *Harpers Weekly* magazine, which he would read and then send to her. He shot several ducks and removed several more frostbitten toes. He would send her more money as soon as he could.

Darling I think of you every hour in the day and do so hope you are comfortable and as near happy as you can be apart. I have been in want of clothes and so have you. I do not care for myself but for you I will try & provide soon. . . . My regards to all and darling I will never leave you again for a field expedition unless you think it best.

He saved the most distasteful news for last, finally telling her about his meeting with Ernst Brenner.

Now darling, I hope you have not made yourself obnoxious . . . for it would only make talk about you and I don't want any of that for your sake. I know you are *in a delicate place, between two fires,* but be careful what you say and think of others. Hear all but say nothing to cause ill feelings. *I do not care to express my opinion here except to neutrals. I will see Brenner before he leaves here about paying him.*

Good night, darling

He wanted to write more, wanted to explain his feelings, but they were too mixed up. He knew his jealousy wasn't warranted, but he couldn't help it. He didn't want to be away from her now, or ever leave her again, but he was excited about traveling west with the Seventh Cavalry and didn't want to leave the Army.

He wasn't sure that buying farmland with his brother was a good idea, wasn't sure he wanted to live so close to his parents. He wasn't even sure he wanted to spend the rest of his life as a farmer and country doctor, not after the excitement and stimulation at Harvard. He knew Fannie would love living in Boston. But would he? One thing he knew for sure. No matter what, he'd always love Fannie.

A week later, he wrote her that the Seventh Cavalry companies at Seward were moving to Fort Lincoln and it appeared the expedition would go out.

He had seen Brenner, who agreed to wait until he returned to settle up his account, *but don't ask him for much money. I will send you half of my pay for April the last of the month. . . . Put my rubbers in the trunk . . . my black covered book on Pathology, Bilroths Surgical Pathology, English Grammar, Huxleys Physiology & such others as you think I will need. . . . I have a case of Pleurisy now under treatment, which is a very serious affair. My toe cases are doing well. . . . I miss you very much. You cannot miss me more but such is Army. It won't be forever. Love and kisses from your loving husband.*

Word came the next day that the rail line to Bismarck was finally open. They would depart the next morning and arrive in Bismarck on April 14, 1876.

10

Bismarck is a squalid dunghill sort of a place, all wooden buildings, broken board walks on the front street. It is on prairie ground on the margin of a bluff. The flats of the Missouri extend back about one mile to this bluff. . . . Took a walk up main street (there is only one side to it.)

—April 16 letter from James to Fannie

A man with his pants around his ankles and white buttocks facing the train welcomed them with a wave and a lurid grin as they neared Bismarck. Urine arched in front of him to the amusement of his comrades.

"Black Hillers," Calhoun spat, "just as soon rob you as do an honest day's work."

The gold seekers' scattered camps grew to a squalid jumble at the outskirts of town; the air stunk of trash fires, rotting garbage, urine and manure. It was a male camp, James noted, but there were a few women. One hung clothes outside a laundry tent. Two women in front of another tent offered carnal pleasure. A pregnant woman with a toddler underfoot tended a simmering stew.

The train screeched to a halt at Camp Hancock in Bismarck. Outside, heavily armed men pushed and jostled in the dusty street and on the boardwalk. A teamster fired two shots skyward and yelled, "Git yer asses movin!" He lashed his mules, and the animals bolted into three riders, nearly knocking one horse off its feet. The men turned and glared with hands on pistol butts, but moved aside.

As cavalrymen led their horses off the livestock cars, James thought "this is going to be a mess," and sure enough it was. Terrified animals reared, kicked and screamed; several soldiers sprawled in the dirt; a few horses nearly got away, and more than one man was dragged into the crowd.

Many bystanders laughed and jeered, but a few jumped in to help. Calhoun and two sergeants mounted and cleared a path with quirts and boots. Two more sergeants mounted and followed close behind with pistols drawn, just in case somebody decided to make trouble. Finally, at the edge of town, everyone mounted and rode a winding, dusty trail down the bluffs to the wide, flat Missouri River valley.

"Fort Lincoln's about five miles downstream on the other side of the river," Calhoun told James. "We'll leave the horses behind for now and take a ferry down, although it might be awhile. A Hancock officer told me the ferry's broken down."

James gave orders to his striker, Private Elihu Clear, and left for Camp Hancock to admit his sick soldiers into the hospital. One man was constipated; another had dysentery; a third was seriously ill with pleurisy. James gave the third man morphine, left instructions for the steward and then joined other officers at the Capitol Hotel for supper—leather-tough beef, potatoes and onions fried in rancid lard, and hard bread with coffee. The peach cobbler wasn't bad.

After supper, they elbowed their way down Bismarck's broken boardwalk past saloons, a blacksmith shop, a dry goods store, a bank, the Bismarck Tribune building, a stationery store and two cafes. Horses stood nose-to-nose at the hitching rails. A dance hall barker promised lovely singers, high-kicking dancers, and intimated more.

"Not for me," James said as several officers headed inside.

Calhoun agreed, and he and James headed back to the hotel.

"This is the respectable part of town," Calhoun said. "The really raw places are down where the steamboats dock. There's a collection of shacks across the river from Fort Lincoln, too, hog ranches with charming names like 'My Lady's Bower' and 'Dew Drop Inn. We caution the men, 'Don't drop in.' but of course many do."

They sipped beer in the hotel's quiet saloon and then started back to camp. The night was cool, the valley floor bathed in moonlight. The river glittered, and the western horizon glowed orange-red from prairie fires that *presented a nice sight in the distance,* James wrote Fannie.

The next morning, he was washing biscuit and eggs down with coffee at the hotel when a balding, distinguished-looking man with a bushy mustache approached their table and introduced himself as Doctor Henry Porter, a Bismarck businessman and contract surgeon at Camp Hancock. "I'd like to join you, but I'm having breakfast with a few town leaders. I'd be pleased if you'd all join me for supper this evening at Hancock."

They did, and James showed his appreciation by devouring two large helpings of roast beef, potatoes, gravy and green beans. "Excellent," he patted his stomach, "especially compared with the hotel's fare."

Porter took out his pipe. "Time for my evening walk, care to join me?"

They strolled around the parade ground. "You'll have a grand adventure with Custer," Porter said, exhaling sweet smoke. "I've heard the Yellowstone country is beautiful, and lots of game. I'd apply, but I know you have all your surgeons."

"You know the Army. That could change."

James wrote Fannie that night that everyone was anxious to get across the river to Fort Lincoln. They would have to camp, since the fort's barracks and officers' quarters were full, but *all the difference is that we will not have to board at the hotel. . . . I hope we shall get into our permanent camp tomorrow and mess where our meals are a little better, or at least cost less. I hope darling you are well and having a*

nice time and hope the snow is all off and things looking lovely. . . . I think
we are going to have a nice time this summer.

Bye bye darling, love & kisses from your loving husband

Men worked all night on the ferry and had it ready before reveille. Mist drifted over the water as they rode to the landing.

"We're crossing on that?" James asked, looking at the small paddle wheeler in the Missouri's rough, spring-swollen water.

Calhoun laughed. "Haven't lost anyone yet, but I guess today could be the day."

The boat settled as the first group boarded. The crew slipped the line, and it raced downstream. It was late afternoon when the ferry labored back for the third and last trip. The morning breeze had increased to a stiff northwest wind, and James heard someone ask the captain if they should wait until morning.

"The wind's no problem!" the captain said.

They spun into the swift current. The boat wallowed in the chop and icy water washed over the sides. Just above the fort, as the bow turned into the current, the captain added steam, the paddlewheel churned and the boat shuddered. James marveled as it edged closer to shore. Crewmen threw lines to men on the bank, who pulled the boat in.

James said a silent prayer of thanksgiving as he jumped into mud.

They made camp two miles south of the fort. Private Clear pitched James's white canvas wall tent and laid planks provided by the quartermaster to make a dry floor. James arranged more boards in a rectangle on top of the planks, packed in straw, and then put his rubber coat and four blankets on top of the straw.

Stretched out on the soft bed, he wrote that his tent was quite cozy. *What I appreciate more than all is the pillow you insisted on my bringing darling. I remember you every time my eyes rest on it.*

He was about to snuff his candle when Calhoun stopped by.

"Two pistols, standard issue," he said, handing James a wooden box. "Keep 'em loaded and handy. Indians roam the area, and it's crawling with no-goods headed for the Black Hills. We've had pistols stolen from the barracks, ammunition, whatever they can get before they depart for Deadwood.

"Last summer, a patrol found one of 'em stripped naked and staked to the ground on the east side of the river. He'd been sliced open and his innards cooked with hot coals. Indians killed a rancher recently, too, beat his head to mush and took his cattle and horses. So needless to say, it can be dangerous out here."

"How'd your wife do while you were gone in seventy-three and seventy-four?" James asked.

"Worried as much as any woman, I guess, but she did all right. Being Custer's sister, and having the support of Custer's wife and the other cavalry wives at Fort Lincoln helped."

"I wish my wife was here. I worry about her, especially with no other cavalry wives at Totten. But, you know, the weather's been so bad and our finances are, too. The transportation, room and board, I can't afford to send for her."

"Have you provided her power of attorney? She'll need it, you know, if something were to happen to you."

"I thought about it before departing Totten, but I didn't want to worry her."

"You ought to take care of it."

James wrote that night: *Darling, I think you had better make out a power of Attorney. . . . Mr. Brenner can make the paper for you and you had better attend to it at once.* He added that he wished she could have traveled to Fort Lincoln with him. *This will be my last expedition. This dirt & waiting is disgusting. . . . I hope darling you are having nice times now as spring has come.* He told her he longed for her, especially when retiring. He asked her how Mitzdorf was doing. He took out his little accounts booklet and told her he had ninety dollars, but he owed the Lincoln trader twenty-five and needed five a week for meals. He wanted to buy two flannel shirts and a pair of boots before the expedition. He needed to replace the inkwell broken between Totten and Seward, and his washbasin and telescope, which were crushed on the trip to Bismarck. He would send her fifty dollars.

I will send you more as soon as I can. . . . Darling I some expect to get my pay for May & June before I leave here but in case I do not I will manage some way so you are provided for. The band is playing evening hymns, which dear makes me feel so lonely. I hear tonight that Custer will command his regiment, but he has not come yet & I don't believe it. He hoped the rumor was true *because Custer has been out & knows better than them that have not been over the ground.*

◇━◇━◇

Later that week, he examined twenty-two of the expedition's forty Indian scouts and then a black interpreter and guide named Isaiah Dorman, a muscular man with salt and pepper hair and a friendly, open face.

"You're a welcome sight, and breath of fresh air, after those Indians," he told Dorman, grimacing and waving his hand in front of his nose.

Dorman laughed. "The Arikaras this time of year coat their skin with animal grease and refrain from bathing. The grease turns rancid, but it keeps the biting flies and mosquitoes at bay. It's a scent that takes some getting used to."

"Not something I'll ever get used to," James replied. "Tell me Mister Dorman, you feel up to this expedition?"

"Yes, sir, doc."

"Any complaints—trouble breathing, fever, constipation?"

"Same as most men, nothing I can't abide."

James peered into Dorman's mouth. "Any teeth bothering you?"

"No sir, doc, had one pulled last year."

He listened to Dorman's heart and lungs. "How old are you?"

"Somewhere about fifty-five years."

"And you're married to an Indian I'm told."

"A Sioux named Visible, yes sir. We lived at Standing Rock with Sitting Bull's Hunkpapas. She's with them now, out where we're headed. I'm hoping to find her and my two boys and bring them back with me."

"You worked for McLaughlin at Devils Lake, didn't you?"

"Rode with him from St. Paul to Devils Lake in seventy-one, was his guide and interpreter, cut wood and took care of the oxen, then stayed for awhile and cut wood for the agency and Army," Dorman replied.

"What would you think about going back to Totten after the expedition?"

"Fine by me, Doc. Like I said, we were living at Standing Rock, but Devils Lake's my wife's people's reservation."

James wrote Fannie that night about examining Indian scouts, describing the task as *not a very nice job*. He also told her about Dorman.

I hope you are content and happy. If you like, you can send & have you a servant sent up & keep house as soon as you like. I saw Ella at Seward and asked her if she would like to go back to Totten next winter. She said she would to live with Mrs DeWolf. I asked her to send you her address and that I thought you would send for her.

There is a Negro man on the expedition who wants to go there with me when I come back, so if you don't want or cannot get Ella or some other good girl, then let me know in time & when I come back I will bring one man or woman as you choose from Lincoln.

He put the letter aside and went to a campfire where Captain Frederick Benteen was holding court. James liked the confident officer, whose cutting wit and irreverent manner reminded him of McDougall. Benteen poured whiskey into a metal cup and handed it to James. "Have you met Doctor Stein? He looks after the mules!"

"Then he's not a doctor," James said stiffly.

"There's not much difference really." Stein spoke loudly with a thick German accent and pumped James's hand. "We treat the same organs and ailments, just in different animals."

"I believe you shoot sick beasts. I've never shot a patient." As Stein continued his discourse about medical doctors and veterinarians, James sat down between Benteen and the scout Lonesome Charley Reynolds, and pointedly ignored the veterinarian.

Heavy rain and steamy heat hatched swarms of mosquitoes, making life miserable for everyone but the greased Arikaras. During evening dress parade, Seventh Cavalry band members stood with instruments in hand, suffering the onslaught while officers' wives observed from the large porch of the Custers' vacant home.

"Look at 'em in their wool dresses," Calhoun said as he and James waited for the evening concert, "bundled in this heat from head to toe with nets over their faces, scarves around their necks, gloved hands and newspapers wrapped around their ankles."

The band started an Italian march. James slapped a gorged mosquito, smearing blood on his cheek. "I wish my wife was up there looking comical along with yours."

He wrote her that the heat, mosquitoes and waiting were getting tiresome. He couldn't wait to get started. *I will be leaving the old Missouri behind and hope we shall be successful in finding some of the cussed Indians that have been the cause of the expedition.*

Fort Lincoln's soldiers left their quarters on May 9 and joined James and the other cavalrymen in camp. The Custers and Major General Alfred Terry arrived on the evening of May 10, *a dreadful hot day*. A battery saluted their arrival, and the generals and Custer's wife spent the night in Custer's grand fort home.

The next morning, Custer entered the camp to uproarious cheers, leading his small procession like a conquering Roman warrior on his prancing horse Dandy. His wife Libbie followed in a carriage, ahead of an ambulance carrying their camping gear and their black cook, Mary.

Custer, sporting dress blues with gold braid, a bright red kerchief and gray hat, waved to the troops with yellow gauntlets. "Men of the Seventh Cavalry, I salute you!" Another wave of cheers filled the air.

McDougall followed with his Louisiana company. "Doctor DeWolf," he smiled, "I made it after all. It's good to see you, my friend!"

"How is Missus M?" James asked.

"She likes Shreveport. It reminds her of her South Carolina home. Your wife?"

"Doing fine, enjoying the Dakota spring."

After the evening band concert, James went to the trader's store and bought a raincoat and rubber pants.

I have two dollars left of my April pay. Of course darling, I waste some . . . but you need not caution me about cards, for I am not so forgetful, for really darling I despise gambling. If it was not for you, dearest, it might be different. . . . Well, it is long after taps & I hear the raise two dollars in a tent close by. I will close for tonight

Happy dreams, darling, good night.

He drew his pay for May and June the next day and sent one month's pay to his brother, Erastus, for the farm. He sent fifty dollars to Fannie and kept seventy-five for himself.

On May 14, he wrote Fannie that he'd been assigned to the right wing under Major Marcus Reno and was enjoying spending time with Reno's adjutant, Second Lieutenant Benjamin Hodgson. Doctor Porter was taking the place of a contract surgeon who didn't want to go on the expedition and had been assigned to Reno's wing, too.

Well darling, I suppose I could change off & not go, but I want very much to go and expect we shall have a good time or as good as can be had in the field.

The expedition was supposed to depart the next morning, but it rained buckets, leaving the heavy wagons hopelessly mired.

11

During the first six or seven months frequent and gentle exercise in the open air and domestic occupation which requires moderate exertion, are very desirable; both have a beneficial influence on the health of the mother, and through her, upon the child.

—"Hints to Mothers for the Management of Health During the Period of Pregnancy, and in the Lying-In Room" by Thomas Bull, M.D.

Fannie puked sour brown coffee and biscuit into a kitchen pot, wiped her face and smiled.

Her X's on their bedside calendar counted for more now—not just the days since James left but the days of her pregnancy as well. She would do everything in her power, she vowed, to make sure that she and her child, their child, would emerge from pregnancy and childbirth healthy and strong.

Sitting down in her favorite chair, she picked up Doctor Thomas Bull's book about the health of mothers and babies during and after pregnancy. It was a book she knew well for she had studied and summarized it for James in Boston. She skimmed quickly to refresh her memory:

Let the bowels be regulated, keeping them slightly relaxed with castor-oil . . . and if this is effected, no other medicine will be necessary. She already had a bottle, and already took a spoonful every day.

It is imagined by some . . . that during this condition a larger proportion of food is necessary than at any other time, the support and nourishment of the child demanding the extra supply. This is a great mistake, for gaining excess weight can endanger the health of both mother and child. *Let the diet, then, be light in kind, moderate in quantity* and *taking sparingly of meat.*

Fannie read with a knowing smile that many women develop an aversion to meat and prefer fruits and vegetables. *Under these circumstances, let her adopt this diet; it is best for her. At the same time I would advise that, occasionally, but with due care, a little fresh meat or game should be taken.* She found meat disagreeable now, but figured she could continue eating a little during evening meals with the Fergusons.

Sleep in a large and airy room, with little clothes about the person, to prevent the accumulation of too much heat. No problem there, not in her "naturally ventilated" quarters.

Rise early. Use the salt-water shower or sponge-bath every morning. . . . Take considerable, but regular, exercise fifteen to thirty minutes every morning after bathing *but never to fatigue . . . in the early months, with a gradual approach to a state of repose as the period of confinement approaches.*

She would walk around the parade ground or down to Brenner's store as often as possible. Pushing Jimmie in his carriage would give her an excuse for some of her walks. She'd continue helping Edna with cooking and cleaning, of course, since her friend was still weak from her birthing travails. She would continue to help the hospital matrons with their chores, too.

Crowded assemblies of all kinds, including large parties, should be avoided. *From neglect of this precaution, miscarriage is a very frequent occurrence among young married women . . . more particularly when they become pregnant for the first time. The visiting, the large dinner parties, immoderate dancing . . . by exhausting the system, produce this accident as the inevitable result.*

Fannie was expected to attend the Saturday dances, but everyone knew she would not dance during James's absence, and no one would question her desire to leave early.

A teetotaler, she agreed with Bull's admonition against alcohol consumption during pregnancy. It should be avoided for the health of both mother and baby. Drinking alcohol for medicinal purposes *has created the solitary drunkard* in many cases and has been known to cause the premature death of a good wife and mother.

The *two grand causes* of *giving birth to puny children are poor diet and spirit drinking, drinking being the most harmful of the two.*

Satisfied, Fannie closed the book and drifted off to warm thoughts of James.

◦▬◦▬◦

As time passed, Fannie's distaste for rancid pork and tough beef increased until the meats were barely tolerable, which posed a problem. She wanted to keep her pregnancy private, wanted James to be the first to know.

Could she keep her secret until he returned, hopefully in mid-July or early August? She would have to. Could she repress her growing aversion to meat? She would have to do that, too.

The leathery, gristly beef wasn't too bad. She cut small bites and swallowed them quickly. The fat-laden salt pork was another matter. It wasn't long before she was muffling gags with her napkin after two or three bites, and not long after that before she was catching and hiding bites in her napkin. She took smaller and smaller portions until one night there was hardly any pork on her plate at all, and every bit of it was left untouched.

To Fannie's relief, the Fergusons didn't seem to notice—until one night, after Doctor Ferguson retired to the parlor, Edna picked up Fannie's plate and asked with a knowing look, "Does Doctor DeWolf know?"

Fannie shook her head.

"I presume you will be letting him know soon."

Fannie shook her head again. "I want to tell him in person. If he's back by July or August, I'll be four or five months along. I can hide it until then."

"He'd want to know right away, Fannie. You should," Edna started, but Fannie cut her off with a sharp "No!"

"I don't understand," she started again, but quickly changed the subject. "I have patterns for dresses I made to hide my condition. You'll need at least two or three. We can make them together while my husband's at the hospital."

"That would be most helpful. I purchased fabric and thread for one summer dress back in March, hoping I was with child. I figured I could use my dressmaking skills to alter my old patterns, but using yours would be most helpful. Please, don't tell anyone, not even your husband."

"Your secret is safe with me."

Walking back to her quarters, Fannie felt as if a weight had been lifted from her shoulders. Finally she had someone to share her secret with. But how could she share with Edna and not with James?

She hurried upstairs and picked up her mother-of-pearl hand mirror. Delicately, she lifted the ruby-encrusted gold cross from her blouse and traced each gem with a finger. Once again, she resolved to tell James everything, well, *almost* everything. She took her stationery, inkwell and pen to the dining room table, but time after time the words came out wrong.

<hr />

Fannie was pinning pattern pieces to fabric when the cramping started. She looked up and saw Edna concentrating on cutting, so she massaged her abdomen and went back to pinning. The cramps grew worse.

"I think I'll lie down for a while."

"Is everything okay?" Edna asked.

"Just tired." Fannie forced a smile. "I'll see you for supper."

Hurrying down the boardwalk and up to her bedroom, she

whispered repeatedly, "God, no, please." She was doing everything right. It couldn't be.

She lay down and placed her hands on her stomach. "Please." Finally, she took off her dress and underclothes and found what she feared—dark brown, smelly spots. Packing a cotton cloth between her legs, she curled up under the covers and drifted away until loud knocks brought her back. Edna was calling. Finally, her friend came upstairs.

"Are you all right?" Edna sat on the edge of the bed and put her wrist on Fannie's forehead. "No fever. What's wrong?" She waited a few moments for an answer and then said. "I'll get my husband."

"No!" Fannie gripped Edna's arm. "I'll be fine. It's just an upset stomach. Go ahead with supper without me."

When the cramps eased a bit, Fannie went downstairs and got Doctor Bull's text.

Leafing frantically, she found passage after passage that made her heart sink: *Many women suppose that the condition of the mind of the mother has no influence upon the physical or mental constitution of the unborn child, and that violent passion, long-continued anxiety, sudden fear . . . are in no way productive of serious consequences.* Any serious mental disturbance *will tell upon the future constitutional vigour and mental health of her offspring.* A sudden *gust of passion* or any *violent emotion* can lead to miscarriage. *Violent mental emotions are capable of disturbing the organs . . . and so producing miscarriage. It is notorious that our physical condition is affected by the state of the mind. In the peculiarly sensitive condition of the pregnant woman, any extraordinary excitement, or depression, especially when produced suddenly, may therefore give rise to the evil of which I am speaking.*

Could she have killed their baby with her fears, grief and melancholy after James's departure? He had died in the storm; she was so sure of it that she experienced terrifying nightmares. Even after she'd learned he'd made it safely to Fort Seward, her fears continued. He still might be killed by Indians.

She turned to the chapter about the prevention of miscarriage. *Can the female herself contribute in any measure to avert her liability to it? . . . In the majority of cases . . . I confidently reply in the affirmative; and it is because the success of such a plan depends for the most part upon the prudence and perseverance of the patient . . . for a medical man can do little to arrest a miscarriage when the process is once set up—that she ought to be fully acquainted with the means of prevention.*

Fannie turned the page.

If the expectant mother has experienced cramping, *followed by the discharge of more or less blood, a partial separation of the child has already taken place. If the pains in the loins and hips increase, becoming sharper . . . with a free discharge of clotting bright-colored blood, the child is altogether separated.*

Her cramps weren't getting worse, which meant partial separation, not too late. She had spotting, but no free flow of clotting blood. She could save their baby. While Bull had admonished expectant mothers to avoid all alcohol consumption, she now read that a glass of wine at night, at least twice a week, might arrest a miscarriage in its early stages. Taking sulfate of iron, sulfate of quinine and extract of gentian might help, too.

Fannie was in bed when Edna checked on her that evening.

"I think it's just emotional exhaustion, from James leaving and not knowing for so long if he survived the storm, and now not knowing what will happen with the Indian campaign. Normally I don't drink at all, as you know, but my husband sometimes gave me a glass of wine in the evening, to settle my nerves. It helped, but I don't have any here."

Edna brought her beef broth simmered with carrots and onions along with the wine.

Later, when Fannie felt sure no one would be out and about, she slipped into the hospital dispensary and found the sulfate compounds but not any gentian. She took the medicine and got into bed. Her cramps grew worse, but she ignored them, certain that the wine and sulfates would protect her. The new cloth between her legs grew wet and warm. Light headed, she drifted off.

"Fannie, you're white as a ghost!" Edna sat on the edge of the bed, felt the moist warmth and gasped at the large, red stain when she pulled back the covers. "I'll get my husband."

Fannie heard Edna through a fog of indifference. Days and nights passed, she wasn't sure how many. Light-headed and drowsy from her massive loss of blood, she drifted in and out of sleep. Edna nursed her back to the point where she had enough strength to sit up and sip broth.

"You know, Fannie, you've lost the baby."

Fannie nodded. "Please, no one must know."

"You needn't be concerned. Doctor Ferguson and I agree, this is a matter between you and your husband."

"Before you leave, would you bring me my stationery, inkwell and pen? They're in the table by my parlor chair."

Knowing she couldn't write James about her pregnancy and miscarriage, Fannie tried to write something cheerful. Instead, her pen poured her misery onto the page. She'd been bedridden for days, she wrote. *I think I cannot survive until you return. I am hardly able to sit up.* He would be heartsick, she knew, but she addressed an envelope and sealed the letter inside. She gave it to Edna the next morning.

"The carrier leaves later this morning. I'll make sure he has it." She smiled and squeezed Fannie's hand. "You look better. How do you feel?"

Fannie didn't answer.

Fannie regained her health and strength and pulled herself out of her depression. Her heavy burden of guilt persisted at first, then faded imperceptibly until one morning she awoke with the realization that maybe her miscarriage was for the best. Her pregnancy was never meant to be, and now James wouldn't have to know. He would return from his campaign and they would talk about their future. She would express her feelings, and she would listen to him. She would be open to everything—children or no children, a medical practice in Boston or farming and a country practice in Pennsylvania. She would even consider what she knew he wanted most—a career in the Army.

She wrote James that she was feeling much better. "Missus Ferguson and I walked down to the lake after supper yesterday. The water was deep blue with a bright splash of orange before the falling sun. The hills around the fort are beautiful, James, covered with white, yellow, purple and blue wildflowers. Are they the same where you are? The other wives say it will be lovely in the fall here when the trees above the lake splash the hills with bright colors. We'll walk arm-in-arm down to the lake, my darling, and ride into the hills as we so often did in Oregon."

Your letter was a balm to me, James replied *You seem content and happy, which I hope you are, then my trip will be bearable.*

12

From the hour of breaking camp, before the sun was up, a mist had enveloped everything. Soon the bright sun began to penetrate this veil and dispel the haze, and a scene of wonder and beauty appeared. The cavalry and infantry . . . the scouts, pack mules, and artillery, all behind the long line of white-covered wagons, made a column altogether some two miles in length. As the sun broke through the mist a mirage appeared, which took up about half of the line of cavalry, and thenceforth for a little distance it marched, equally plain to the sight on the earth and in the sky.
    —Elizabeth B. Custer, in her book "Boots and Saddles"

Light sifted through fog in the river valley, urging a predawn chorus from waking birds. Bugles blared, and James fell in with Reno's staff behind Custer. Over a thousand cavalry and infantrymen, a hundred wagons, a long pack train and a large cattle herd followed.

Deep male chants and high-pitched female trills greeted them to the beat of loud drums as they approached the Indian scouts' camp. Closer to the fort, native voices gave way to the wails and cries of enlisted men's wives, sweethearts, babies and toddlers.

James felt a shiver when the Seventh Cavalry band struck up a brassy rendition of *Garryowen* as they entered the fort. Custer saluted Terry, the expedition's commander, as they passed in review.

Behind Terry, cavalry officers' wives watched stoically from the large porch of the Custers' quarters, silently shedding tears. James thought of Fannie on that frigid day when he left her at Totten— sixty-eight long days had passed and her icy tears were still frozen in his memory.

The band struck up *The Girl I Left Behind Me* as they left the fort and rode west into hills, and James recalled his own version of the soldiers' favorite farewell song:

> *I'm lonesome since I crossed the hill,*
> *And o'er the moor and valley,*
> *Such heavy thoughts my heart do fill,*
> *Since parting with my Fannie.*
>
> *I'll seek no more the fine and gay,*
> *For each but does remind me,*
> *How swift the hours did pass away,*
> *With the girl I left behind me.*

Near the crest of the hills, he turned in his saddle and saw the mirage witnessed by many that day—ghostly apparitions of mounted men floating above themselves in the lifting fog. The sight sent another shiver down his spine.

They slogged twelve miles through mud and camped on a high bank overlooking the Heart River. James and Porter sat and watched the sun sink at the prairie's edge.

"Seems like there's no end to it," James said.

"No limit to the opportunities, either. Bismarck will be a center of commerce long after the gold seekers are gone. There'll be room for more than one doctor, plenty of business opportunities, too, and land for ranching."

James liked Porter, liked the west's wide open spaces, too. He could sell the Pennsylvania farmland back to his brother or parents and then either stay in the Army or start a ranch and establish a medical practice out here. Wouldn't that be nice.

He'd renew his contract for another year in October, and maybe Fannie would change her mind about moving back east. Maybe the excitement of a new land, and new opportunities, would grab her, too.

The grass flashed orange in the evening breeze. Men laughed and smoked. James retired to his tent and enjoyed a guitar's soft chords and singing while he wrote Fannie:

I am glad to get out for now every day counts. . . . .I am enjoying the march first-rate & expect we shall have a nice time as can be had in the field. I have my tent put up & taken down, my bed made, horse saddled, etc., and have a quart of nice whiskey in my valise in case of need.

—Camp on Heart River, D.T., May 17th, 1876

It took three hours to cut the river banks away, build a bridge of logs and sod, and move the wagons across the next morning, a preview of scores of tedious crossings ahead. They slogged in mud just ten miles and camped in driving rain. The next morning, James joined Custer at the head of the advance scouting column.

"Lieutenant Calhoun speaks highly of you," Custer said as they rode in heavy rain. "He says he could use some of your wisdom when it comes to cards."

"My wife is a moderating influence," James replied.

"A strong woman is good for a man's career. I gave up drinking for Missus Custer, even though my bachelor brother chides me."

James's horse slipped into Custer's. "This mud's tiresome," he said, trying to move the subject away from soldiers, gambling and drinking.

"Make the most of the day, doctor! That's my creed." Custer kneed Dandy and splashed ahead toward Captain Tom Custer and General Terry. James urged his horse after him, following the river to a rise, where Custer stopped and asked James, "A good camp site, don't you think?"

"Out of the worst of the mud, yes, sir," James replied as the reporter from the Bismarck paper reined his squat mule alongside.

"Tom, can the wagons make it this far?" Custer asked.

"Yep, good place to ford, too," his brother nodded as he pointed ahead where the cut bank dropped and the water rippled in shallows.

The Custers rode down toward the river and James was about to follow when the reporter said, "Doctor Woolsey! I'm Mark Kellogg with the Bismarck Tribune."

"I know who you are."

"I heard General Custer ask you about the camp site. Why would he care what you think?" Kellogg asked, his pen poised to write down the answer.

"You'd have to ask him," James snapped.

"What do you think of General Custer?"

"A fine leader. You don't know who I am, do you," James added curtly.

"A surgeon named Woolsey," Kellogg replied.

"That's what you put in your paper."

"How's that spelled?"

"You should get your facts straight before you put someone's name in the paper." James spurred his horse away, leaving Kellogg and his squat mule behind.

He wrote Fannie that night about his ride with Custer: *If you see the Bushmark Tribune, you can see what a bungle some reporter made. Who is Woolsey? Of course, it meant myself, your Hub.* He could have corrected the reporter, he wrote, but he didn't *because I don't take his trash.* The Tribune describes Custer very well, he conceded, noting that the famous cavalry commander likes to go ahead with the scouts, dressed in his very *fashionable and knobby* buckskin suits. Don't worry about my safety *as we shall not see an Indian this summer. . . . I carry a carbine & revolver so I will be armed in case of need. I think it is nonsense to carry it but I do so want to be sure & get back that I take every precaution to be on the safe side.*

The fourth day out, they spotted Indians watching them from a distance. When a shot rang out a short time later, followed by a shriek, James assumed a soldier had been hit by a sniper. He spurred his horse and found men gathered around a comrade lying in mud. Dropping down beside the man with his medical bag, he found a blood-spattered bullet hole in the back of his boot.

"What's your name, soldier?" he asked in a kindly tone.

"John Connell, sir, trumpeter Company B."

"What happened?"

"Shot myself, sir."

The boot was tight and took some yanking to remove. Men carried Connell, groaning in pain, to an ambulance, where James cleaned and dressed the wound.

When the cavalry reached their next campsite, he rode back to the wagon train and found Connell blue-white and shaking.

"Get this man into dry clothes and pile blankets on him!" he shouted angrily.

"I don't recommend shooting yourself in the heel to get off duty." Connell tried to smile through chattering teeth. "The bouncing is banging my heel to distraction, sir. I'd just as soon be on my horse."

"Not for a month or more," James replied.

◻◼◻◼◻

Sun splashed color across the eastern horizon the next morning, heralding their first day without rain. The wagons still slogged in soft ground but they camped on a hill above the mud. James took a sponge bath, changed into clean clothes, gave his dirty laundry to his orderly, Private Clear, and went to the evening fire, where he filled up on antelope, biscuits and coffee. Full and sleepy, he stretched out and stared at the stars. He'd just about dozed off when Major Reno arrived with news.

"A messenger from General Gibbon says he's camped with his Montana column on the north bank of the Yellowstone opposite the mouth of Rosebud Creek. Gibbon thinks there's a large camp of Sioux and Cheyenne on the Rosebud or Bighorn River, so we'll be joining his forces on the Yellowstone."

"And then go after them damn redskins," someone said.

"General Terry believes if we approach them in good faith, they'll agree to move peacefully with their families back to their reservations. Custer, I think, is spoiling for a fight. No glory for him, no home in the White House, if things end peacefully," Reno said.

James retired to his tent, took a nasty pill for constipation and told Fannie that his nose and ears were nearly burned off. *Well darling, as I have to get up at 2:30 or 3 a.m. tomorrow, I must retire. It is getting chilly as I have taken off my flannel for the night. Love & kisses to my darling wife from your loving husband,*

J.M.D.

They traveled the next day over easy rolling hills in splendid weather and enjoyed band concerts at each stream crossing. James sat down next to McDougall during one stop and found his friend in a foul mood despite the warm sun and music.

"Custer's kept my company riding rear guard through cow shit the whole way. No rotation, no chance to ride at the front. You, on the other hand, I see you're already riding ahead with the general and his chosen few. Congratulations."

"I went on a scout with him, that's all, everyone takes a turn."

McDougall glared at James. "Six or eight officers, the rest he snubs."

"The surgeons rotate. Doctor Porter has been out with him."

"He takes his brothers, relatives by marriage and ass kissers, even that snot-nosed nephew of his. Some of us never go, but I guess you hadn't noticed."

James didn't know what to say. He liked McDougall, considered him a good friend, but he wasn't about to tell him that he, Reno and Benteen might enjoy more favor from Custer if they didn't drink so much.

James and Porter were invited to go hunting with Custer that afternoon, but James stayed in camp. After a nap, he joined several officers at a campfire. McDougall studiously ignored him and devoted all of his attention to Benteen, who was offering snide observations about Custer and his pals. Tired of the sniping, James went to his tent and wrote Fannie about the hunting invitation. He would like to try hunting *but dear I am a little lazy & do not want to have my scalp lifted. . . . I do not think there is any danger yet, but I am going to be on the safe side and stay with the command. . . . The band plays now & every evening & marching out of camp every morning. So we have something to cheer the dashing Cavalier. . . . The trip is not pleasant to some high in rank for several reasons, which I will tell you when I come home.*

He swam and bathed in a pond the next day while the wagons made another crossing. The clear, cold water washed away a week's accumulation of smelly sweat and dirt that a sponge bath couldn't reach. A mail carrier caught up to the expedition and handed out letters that evening. He read that Fannie was bedridden again. Dejected, he sat with his back against a tree and stared at the river's swirling eddies. Finally, he folded the letter and went to his tent.

I am very sorry darling that you are so sick, but hope you will be well when this reaches you. . . . I fear you have worked yourself sick. . . . I do so hope you are well now and am so sorry for you that I cannot be with you. . . . Darling, you must try & have a good time & if you want to, go in the lake, but do not go when there is a wind.

A horse jerked loose from a soldier and splashed wildly across the river. Thunder clapped in the distance. Worried and distracted, James's writing rambled.

I think we are going to have a shower tonight. Shall I get a pony for you when I come in? It has been very hot today. I find I am skipping from one thing to another so rapidly. I guess you will not call this a real good letter. I don't know when I can send you this. It is now expected that we shall reach the Little Missouri Monday night. I don't see much of Terry or Custer. They go in advance & of course I go with my wing commander. Good night darling wife. Love & fond remembrance & hoping so much darling that you are well again.

13

Planting Moon

Word had spread that the desperation of the Sioux was such that they were forced to eat their own horses. . . . According to some, the Fort Totten Sioux were on the verge of joining with neighboring Santee Sioux and Hunkpapas. If the Fort Totten Sioux were cared for, "the more remote bands might get the good word and be influenced to settle down . . . ." To accomplish this, the Sioux not only had to be given temporary subsistence to enable them to survive, but had to be taught farming and "civilized" ways in order to become more self-sufficient.

—"Soldiers and Sioux: Military Life Among the Indians at Fort Totten" by J. Michael McCormack

Fannie pulled the sheet and a light blanket up to her chin against the morning chill. Birds chirped, the sky was clear and the air fresh, a beautiful day. Without thinking, she placed her hands on her stomach, and felt a pang of emptiness and regret. No baby, nothing growing inside her anymore. She pushed the feeling away. There would be no more feelings of guilt, no more depressing letters to James.

Wrapped in her robe, she went to the dining room table, covered with maps, and studied his path west. Not that she needed them anymore. She knew every twist and turn in the Heart River, how it dipped south and then wandered northwest to its source just east of Dakota's northern badlands. She knew where he would cross the Little Missouri and then continue west to the Yellowstone, and from there to its tributaries where the Sioux might be camped. She never tired of tracing his path.

It was still cool inside their quarters at mid-day, but the sun's heat soaked through her thin wool coat as she walked to the Fergusons' for dinner. After the meal, she strolled to the lake, where sunlight flashed over ripples. Reclining on her favorite rock, she relaxed in its warmth, closed her eyes and drifted off, thinking of James. She understood why he liked the Army. She'd enjoyed their Oregon adventure, too, the excitement of the wilderness Army camp and the west's wide open spaces.

But while she wanted to remain open-minded, she couldn't see how it would work, especially if there were children, and there probably would be. Farming and managing a country medical practice together in a settled and civilized place would be best for them and their children. Perhaps, if he couldn't stand the idea of living near his parents, he would agree to sell their land to his family and they could move back to Boston.

She was almost asleep, drifting away from her thoughts, when Marie's voice startled her. "I thought I might find you here."

They stared at the water without another word until Fannie finally, asked, "Do you remember last November, the first time we rode out to the reservation, you started to say something about the Indians and farming and your husband interrupted you?"

Marie smiled. "I remember that your husband interrupted you several times, too, especially when you asked questions about rations going to the fort trader. Our husbands don't always like us speaking our minds."

"What were you going to say?" Fannie asked.

"I spent my first fourteen years living with my Dakota Sioux family in Minnesota. My parents sent me to a white school in Wisconsin in eighteen fifty-six, so I was away when Inkpaduta and his Dakota band killed settlers in Iowa in eighteen fifty-seven. I was living in the white world during the Dakota uprising in Minnesota, too.

"White settlers suffered grievously at the hands of the Indians during those troubled times. But I lived with the Dakota people and saw them suffer years of thievery and exploitation before the uprising. Their land was stolen and then the agents and traders cheated them out of their rations and money. Worst of all, they lost their dignity to the whiskey vendors.

"I tried to explain these things to my husband, so he could see both worlds, both cultures, as I do. It was no use. He sees only the white way and complains about Indian stubbornness. So he says the Indians refuse to learn how to farm, even though they have been farming for thousands of years. When I remind him, he says their farming methods are primitive."

"They are, aren't they?"

"When I was a girl living with my Dakota grandmother, she and the other women grew corn, squash and beans in what they called Three Sisters gardens. The plants worked together like sisters. The corn stalks stood tall in rich river bottom soil; the bean vines climbed the stalks and the squash vines spread their broad leaves below, keeping weeds out and moisture in.

"The women took pride in their gardens because they fed everyone. Now, my husband and the government say the men must do the farming, even though they are traditionally warriors and hunters, protecting their people and providing them meat. Now, the men have to plow up the dry prairie and plant corn and potatoes in rows. Their crops wither in drought and the soil washes away in heavy rains."

"I've seen many good farms and gardens planted that way," Fannie said.

"It works in many places, for white people, but not so well out here. Even worse, making the men farm takes pride away from them and from the women, too. My husband can't see that. He sees only one way, the white way."

"Why don't we ride out to the reservation? I'd like to see my friends," Fannie said.

"That's why I came looking for you," Marie smiled.

They rode over grassy hilltops and through marshy sloughs muddied by the melt of patchy snow. Wildflowers danced in sprouting buffalo grass. Meadowlarks, killdeer and red-winged blackbirds filled the air with mating songs. Honking geese flew overhead. Ducks paddled on ponds.

"Dakota seemed like the worst place on earth when James and I rode over these hills last November. Now I see why people might come to love this land."

"It is beautiful," Marie said, "but it can be a hard place even this time of year—spring floods then summer's scorching heat and droughts. Last summer grasshoppers swarmed like dark rivers across the sky, sometimes blotting out the sun. They ate every blade of grass, every corn stalk, squash and bean vine, clothing and animal hides. They even chewed on the soldiers' wagon covers and the Indians' tepees."

Marie slowed the agency wagon down a steep hill.

"After the grasshopper plague two years ago, troops spent the winter delivering food and clothing to settlers in Dakota and Minnesota. Over fourteen thousand people got bacon, flour, coats, caps, boots and shoes. The Indians got their usual meager rations."

"I thought the government wanted to pacify the Indians. Wouldn't drought assistance have helped?"

"Congress wants to humble them more than help them. If their ponies die, they can't ride. If they're starving, they can't fight."

"The Indians out where my husband is going, I doubt they're too weak to fight."

"They and their ponies probably have plenty to eat, but it won't be that way for long. I fear for them."

"I confess my fears are for my husband."

As they crossed into reservation land, Marie said, "I was hoping you would ride out with me today. I wanted to be out here when I gave you my bad news."

Fannie frowned.

"This reservation is my home now. Beckwith fired me two days ago and fired my husband yesterday."

Marie stated it so softly Fannie wasn't sure she'd heard her right. "What?"

"He accused me of turning the Indians against him and accused my husband of stealing agency food and supplies. He ordered us out of our agency quarters and banned my husband from the reservation." Smiling bitterly, she added, "He neglected to ban me, so I've moved in with a family in Little Fish's camp so I can look after my husband's interests."

"Where is your husband?"

"On his way to Jamestown, and from there to St. Paul to demand Beckwith's dismissal and to seek his appointment," Marie replied as they neared Little Fish's camp. "If Beckwith isn't dismissed and my husband appointed, who knows what will happen. Beckwith followed through with his threats and cut rations, even though I don't believe he has permission yet from Washington. Polygamists and their families are getting less than half their ration, so are families who haven't kept their children in school. Nearly every family's affected.

"Many Braves have gone hunting off the reservation to find meat for the families, but hide hunters have taken most of the buffalo. The deer and elk are almost gone, too. When Beckwith found out, he cut the hunters' rations even more. Arousing Hawk is one of the punished hunters, so he, Walks Behind and Caske have almost nothing now. Little Fish and Wenonah share what little they have."

Thin wisps of smoke curled from Little Fish's tepee. They found Walks Behind inside, holding Caske. The boy smiled when he saw Fannie and extended his arms. She sat down and took him in her arms, clutching him closely as if she could press nourishment into his birdlike, thin body. Gaunt and hollow-eyed, Walks Behind looked at Fannie and whispered in her native tongue.

"Her breasts have dried up," Marie translated. "All they have left is bones boiled in water and a little sugar, coffee and flour."

Little Fish slept with a blanket over his legs. Wenonah went outside. Walks Behind spoke and Marie translated again. "Arousing Hawk has gone hunting again. He had no choice. The meat isn't much, usually just a couple squirrels, a rabbit or maybe a raccoon, every now and then a deer."

"We must do something; we can't allow this," Fannie said.

"As long as Beckwith's in charge, I don't know what," Marie replied.

Wenonah returned with two bowls of cracked-bone soup and offered them to Marie and Fannie. Fannie shook her head with wet eyes and motioned for Wenonah or Walks Behind to eat it. Marie refused, too. The proud grandmother spooned several spoonfuls into Caske's mouth and then went out and poured the rest back into the pot.

"We have to do something," Fannie repeated. "We have to get them food."

"There is none." Marie paused. "Well, there's food, plenty of it in the agency storehouse, but Beckwith wouldn't let us give it to the Indians."

"Is the storehouse guarded?"

"Yes, by Indian police who follow Beckwith's orders."

<hr />

Conditions deteriorated rapidly until most families' diets consisted of boiled bones, roots and grass. The Indians in Beckwith's police force had flour, sugar and a little meat, but even they and their families were suffering. Families began leaving the reservation, a trickle at first and then a swelling stream until one day Fannie and Marie rode into the camp closest to the fort and found only circles of hard-packed ground where tepees had stood. The few Indians left were preparing to leave.

"Everyone's leaving—either north toward the Turtle Mountains, where they hope to find game, or southwest to the Standing Rock Reservation, where they hope they'll be given food," a woman told them as she loaded a travois.

They rode at a lope to Little Fish's camp, where the chief's tepee stood alone.

Wenonah greeted them. "Our son and daughters left with their families yesterday. They've all gone north. The boy agent Beckwith is starving us. He told my husband he'd lose all of his rations if he didn't renounce the Medicine dances. And he told him he would no longer be head chief if he ever saw or spoke to you again, Missus McLaughlin. He doesn't seem to realize that everyone is leaving. He's crazy."

"Like a fox," Marie said. "He wants to show his Catholic superiors, who've demanded his resignation, that he can force you to give up your traditions and become true Christians."

"We don't understand your ways or your feuds. We only know we need food," Wenonah replied.

Little Fish stretched his arms out with his eyes closed. When he finished his soft, chanting prayer, he said, "I told our people they should stay. The soldiers will come after them. Our warriors said they would rather die fighting the blue coats now than watch more elders and children die slowly from starvation."

"Settlers will demand blood when they learn about the exodus," Fannie said. "General Hunt's the only one who can stop it."

"And the one who can chase the Indians down," Marie responded with a frown.

"He'll find out soon, anyway, or already knows. I'm going to see him."

"Do what you must. I'll stay with Little Fish and Wenonah."

Fannie found General Hunt fuming in his study. He already knew about Beckwith's draconian measures and the Indian exodus.

"Can't you do something?" Fannie asked. "Maybe reason with Beckwith? If he agrees to restore the Indians' rations, I'm sure they'll return peacefully."

Hunt stared at the wall behind Fannie, as if he hadn't heard a word she'd said, and then his face flushed beet red. Exploding from his desk, he grabbed his hat and charged out like a mad bull.

Fannie was right behind when the commander found Beckwith at the trader's store.

"Your reservation's empty! Did you know that?" The war veteran jerked Beckwith out of his chair by the stove. Beckwith broke free, knocked over a barrel of flour in his retreat and fell into the powder.

Hunt jerked him up. "I will not allow you to starve the Indians into acts of desperation!" He pushed him against a wall and let him go. "Brush yourself off!" Flour billowed from Beckwith's clothes. "Early tomorrow," Hunt said, "Chief Little Fish and an Army escort will take you to the other chiefs and their bands. You will inform them that they remain in charge and that you have rescinded *all* of your ration cuts. If you refuse, you will be jailed for endangering everyone in this territory."

"You can't do that!"

Hunt flushed a deeper crimson and started for the agent.

"Yes, general!"

"Report to the stables at eight hundred."

Beckwith scurried off to his quarters and with a shaking hand penned his resignation, dated April 29 and effective July 1. It was addressed to Charles Ewing, Commissioner of the Catholic Bureau of Indian Missions. He'd fulfilled his promise to Ewing to submit his resignation but craftily extended his stay and pay for two months.

Beckwith restored the Indians' rations, but the bug-infested flour, hard sugar and spoiled meat barely kept them alive. The agent holed up in his house and sent word that Indians with grievances would have to make appointments to see him at his office. The proud chiefs refused, so week after week, wagons loaded with seeds and implements for spring planting sat in the agency barn.

One day in early June, Marie told Fannie that her husband had been appointed to replace Beckwith as Devils Lake Indian Agent but he feared his Congressional confirmation would be held up by Beckwith's Washington allies.

She showed Fannie a copy of a letter her husband had sent

Ewing, asking for his *kind assistance in having my appointment ratified...as soon as possible* because of the deplorable condition of the Indians. *Major Smith, Post Paymaster, U.S.A., and Dr. Ferguson, Post Surgeon . . . arrived here last evening, and tell me that there is but little being done by the Indians this spring. . . . This neglect of planting will be greatly felt next winter, when our Indians depend upon their produce for at least one half of their subsistence.*

Fannie called on Hunt the next morning and showed him the letter. "If they don't start planting soon, they won't have vegetables next winter."

"I'm aware of the situation, but Mister Beckwith, as much as I dislike the man, still runs the agency. Beyond getting the Indians' rations restored, there's not much I can do."

"You could have men standing by to protect Mister Beckwith while the Indians get the seeds and implements they need."

"What you're suggesting could have serious repercussions. If Mister Beckwith tries to stop them . . ." He didn't finish the thought. "The Indians must come unarmed, and only the number needed to drive the wagons and herd the oxen. I must know exactly when they will arrive."

Fannie and Marie met with Little Fish, who shook his head with his arms crossed. "If there's trouble, the soldiers will shoot us, not the boy agent."

"General Hunt will make sure there's no trouble," Fannie said.

"I know he means what he says," Little Fish said, "but if there is trouble, it will be Indians who are killed."

"If you don't do this," Marie said, "your people will starve."

Little Fish stared up at the sky, closed his eyes for several minutes, then opened them and nodded.

At the arranged time, Fannie and Marie waited on a ridge with a view of the agent's house and agency barn. Beckwith's wife gave the first signal. Outside hanging laundry, she dropped a white shirt into her basket and ran shouting to the house. Beckwith stormed out a moment later and ran toward the barn. Soldiers blocked him.

"What are you doing? Let me pass!"

"We're here to protect you, General Hunt's orders. The Indians are collecting what they need for planting. We'll see they do it peacefully."

Beckwith made a move to get around the soldiers. They moved with him. "Get out of my way!"

"Respectfully, sir, there will be no confrontation or contact between you and the Indians. That is our orders."

Beckwith stormed back to his house.

Fannie sipped honey-sweetened tea in her parlor that evening, reflecting on the day's events. She'd helped the Indians and bested Beckwith in the bargain. She smiled then sobered. James wouldn't approve.

What would he have done? Maybe he would have found a less confrontational way to resolve the problem. Or maybe he wouldn't have done anything and the Indians would have had less to eat next winter.

Her thoughts turned to their last night together, warm thoughts, and then an empty longing and feelings of guilt.

14

Badlands

The valley of the river averages about one mile in width, hemmed in on both sides by impassable Bad Lands. The river is crooked beyond description . . . we found the Little Missouri River so crooked and the Bad Lands so impassable that in marching fifty miles today we forded the river thirty-four (34) times. The bottom is quicksand.

—Letter from George Armstrong Custer to his wife, Elizabeth, May 30, 1876

They camped in grassland amid eroded spires and stepped buttes scattered like chess pieces in a half-finished game. Badlands cropped above them to the south. To the north, their plateau overlooked an endless maze of gullies and ravines twisting around colorful formations. James and Porter joined a group of officers at the edge.

"I can't imagine traveling through that," James said, wiping his brow.

"You don't have to imagine it. We'll be in badlands like that tomorrow," Calhoun replied.

The cavalry band struck up a waltz at the foot of a large hill, striated in soft shades of red, yellow, gray and brown. Teamsters turned their covered wagons and parked in parallel rows. Men pitched tents in a circle with Custer and Terry's large hospital tents commanding high ground at the western edge. The Indian scouts camped farther west, near the divide above the Little Missouri.

Supper was late, and James was hungry. He consumed double portions of antelope ribs, biscuits, peas and peach cobbler. Wiping his hands on his pants, he patted his stomach with satisfaction, and walked back to the edge of the cliff.

Blue shadows lengthened in front of the buttes and hills as the big, orange sun slipped in and out of smoke-gray clouds. Harmonica notes, guitar chords and soft singing floated over the grassland.

Tired from the long day on the trail, James watched the sun slip away and then retired to his tent, removed his boots and socks and rubbed his hot feet. He wrote Fannie that the *days are getting pretty hot & the horses get stuck up with wild cactus & then don't they bound and make it merry for their riders. . . . It is sometimes fun to see a company march through a bed of it. My horse has not had the luck to get caught yet.*

Bye darling, love & kisses from your loving husband, James M DeWolf

He tried to sleep but sour gas boiled and his stomach churned. After a couple hours of tossing and turning, he put on his boots and went outside. The moon was bright, stars glittered like diamonds, and the tents, grass, buttes and spires glowed pale white.

He felt a swell of emotion, remembering how his jealousy had spoiled a night when northern lights shimmered and the moon and stars made the snow sparkle around Fort Totten. Fannie glowed that night, too. She'd had such a good time at the dance, and had been dazzled by the shimmering colors and starry sky. He'd ruined it.

He walked through calf-high grass past a sentry post to the edge of the cliff. The wasteland stretched below in fantastic patterns of white light and black shadow. Sitting with his back against crumbling clay, he let his mind wander through dark passages and over bright peaks—the adrenaline-driven excitement and horrors of war, the rapture of courtship and marriage, the stimulating challenges of medical school, his insecurities and regrets, his fears and hopes, and always his enduring love of Fannie. No matter where his thoughts wandered, they found their way back to Fannie—her beauty, her tender love for him, her spunk and fire. She was everything to him. Why did he treat her badly sometimes? Why did he offer stupid advice in his letters? He had no reason for his jealous insecurity, no reason to chastise her.

"Excuse me, sir?"

James's hand jumped to his holster.

"Sorry, didn't mean to startle you, sir." It was his orderly Elihu Clear, a boyishly handsome man with blue eyes and light hair. "I couldn't sleep and saw you leave your tent."

"Indigestion?" James asked.

"No, sir."

"These badlands are something, aren't they?"

"Yes sir they are," Clear replied, squatting at a respectful distance.

"You've been with Custer and the Seventh Cavalry quite awhile. You were in the Washita Campaign in sixty-eight against the Cheyenne, weren't you?"

"Yes, sir, whipped them devils, taught 'em a lesson."

"A great victory for the Seventh."

"Yes, sir. Them Cheyenne was camped in Injun Territory an' goin' up an' committin' depredations in Kansas—burnin' cabins an' travelers' wagons, slaughterin', torturin', mutililatin'. They kidnapped an' ravaged good, Christian women, too, found one with her baby dead in their camp, shot twice in the head an' her baby's face bashed in, looked like she was trying to escape with her child during the fight."

They stared at the moon-lit landscape for several minutes.

"There are things I try to forget. When I can't, I get up an' walk, like tonight," Clear muttered. He spat between his feet and stared out over the wasteland. "We killed over a hundred of them devils, most of 'em, it turned out, women, children an' old folks. Don't bother me none, them bein' savages, an' everybody knowin' the only good Injun's a dead Injun." Clear paused again and nervously cleared his throat. "Everybody was slappin' me on the back and congratulatin' me cuz I was the one what killed Chief Black Kettle's daughter." He picked up a pebble and tossed it. "Saw an Injun runnin' for the river an' shot. Didn't know it was a squaw 'til I run up to make sure the Injun was dead an' looked at her face. She was pretty, not like no savage, but I still felt good, and did for some time. Then I started seeing her face in the muddy snow in my sleep."

"In the heat of battle," James began, but Clear wasn't listening. "All I saw was an Injun runnin', didn't know it was a squaw."

"You did your duty."

"I know, sir, but I still see her face."

● ○ ●

They traveled in blazing heat and choking dust the next day. The following day, they made camp by the Little Missouri and Custer led four companies upstream to investigate rumors that a large band of Sioux was camped in the badlands.

James rode at the head of the column with the general, his brother Captain Tom Custer, nephew Autie Reed, the *Tribune* reporter and the scouts. Looking around, he realized there was some truth to what McDougall said about Custer and his favorites, but what could he do?

The valley was narrow with endless bends, oxbow ponds, mud holes and soupy flats. Horses mired and fell. Several hours into the ride, Custer's nephew flew off his falling horse and landed head-first in a pool of watery sand. Buried nearly to his waist, his legs flailed, the pool jiggled like gelatin and everyone laughed; Custer guffawed loudest of all.

Then Tom Custer asked, "Shouldn't we get him out?"

"The boy has to learn to fend for himself!" Custer replied.

"He's drowning!" Tom Custer yelled.

"He's still kicking! But if you're *worried*, help him," Custer said.

Tom Custer flushed and hesitated. No one was laughing any more. "Get him out of there!"

Two men jumped from their horses and sunk past their knees.

Several more jumped in and helped pull Reed out. He lay on his side and convulsively choked but drew no air.

James jumped from his horse, stuck two fingers into Reed's mouth and cleared his throat. Quickly, he scooped out more muddy sand, slapped Reed's back and pushed on his chest. Reed gagged, choked water and sand down his windpipe, then coughed and heaved. Loud laughter erupted and then shouts of encouragement.

James looked up, amazed. No one seemed to realize that Custer's nephew had almost died.

"Good work, doctor," Custer said.

Reed stumbled to his feet and staggered with a daffy smile.

"Autie, I expect from here on you'll watch the mud holes!" Custer shouted.

Reed grinned. "Yes sir, general. Watch out for mud holes!"

"Move out!" Custer said.

The river twisted like a running snake. More horses and riders struggled and fell, but James's plodding giant made it with no trouble.

"Far enough!" Custer said. "There aren't any Indians up here!" He turned to Tom Custer and added quietly, "I thought the rumors were nonsense, but General Terry insisted we take a look."

"We forded the river thirteen times general," James told Custer.

"We made seventeen crossings in twenty-five miles," Custer replied. He pointed to a high butte. "We'll take a look from up there and head back."

A well-worn trail led to the top. Bloody Knife, Custer's favorite Indian scout, said it had been made by Indians but hadn't been traveled for some time.

James found a secluded spot near the northern edge and ate alone, lost in thoughts that twisted, turned, disappeared and reappeared like the river below. Would Fannie resist another year at Totten? Would she go along? If she did, would she enjoy it enough to want to stay in Dakota? Or would she hold him to their plans for a farm and private practice in Pennsylvania.

For the first time, he realized with certainty that he didn't want to live near his parents. When he was growing up, his mother was domineering and he couldn't do anything right in his father's eyes. It was a relief, getting away when he was seventeen.

He remembered the wonderful times he and Fannie had in Oregon. No children, no farm or medical practice to worry about, just the two of them working together in the hospital. When he got back to Totten, they would ride together over rolling prairie and through timbered hills the way they did in Oregon. She would work in the hospital, too, and help him in the Indian camps. Would it take her back to their romantic times in Oregon? He didn't know.

He wrote to her that night about their ride up the Little Missouri and Custer's nephew's close call.

Well my darling I hope you are well again. Give my regards to all. I think of you every day & shall be careful of myself if need should be but do not expect there will be any occasion. Love & kisses darling from your loving Husb., J.M. DeWolf.

◦ ◦ ◦ ◦

Rain swept across the badlands that evening and continued the next day as they rode through slippery ravines and over greasy hills west of the Little Missouri. Icy rain, driven by a cold north wind, increased after supper.

James drifted away to its staccato rhythm and slept soundly until loud thumps jolted him. His mind raced. Was it a bear trying to get in, or a mountain lion? A buffalo stampede? Maybe Indians running from tent to tent, slashing them open with their knives, clubbing sleeping men senseless and taking their scalps?

He grabbed his pistol, untied the front flaps and tried to absorb an incomprehensible scene. His tent and the others were being pelted by big, wet globs of snow! In June!

He put on his hat, raincoat and rubber boots, and stepped outside. Wet snow smacked his face as he scraped a heavy layer off his tent's sagging roof. He went back inside and tried to sleep, but the thumping was too loud. Every now and then, he went back out and scraped the snow off.

It was dark and still snowing when reveille sounded. James put on his raincoat and boots and walked to the campfire area, hoping against hope to find hot coffee. The fire ring was buried under slushy snow. No one else was up.

"I guess I'm the only damned fool in this whole damned camp." He slogged back and dropped into bed, not bothering to remove his wet raincoat and boots. He slept soundly until mid-morning, when Private Clear awoke him.

"Breakfast in half an hour, sir, we're not moving until the weather improves."

James ate hardtack and cold bacon washed down with cold water and slogged back to his tent, where he drank two shots of medicinal whiskey and slept. It snowed all day, partially melted and then refroze.

That evening, he drank scalding coffee by a smoky fire, went back to his tent and wrote in his diary, *Remain in camp all day. Do not move. It is hell and more. Muddy.*

The next morning, he wrote Fannie that it was snowing and they were moving the wagons to the west side of a deep ravine so they'd be ready to get out of the mud and find better grass.

I have a fire in front of my tent and it nearly smokes my eyes out. Now darling I occasionally think how nice a home would be—"be it ever so humble." I think it hard and have a wall tent and all the conveniences possible. How do those take it that have perhaps been reared more tenderly and are now mule driving or are in dog tents. . . . There are only a few of the men that have rubber coats. They get wet and dry themselves by standing around the fires.

He slept until late afternoon, got up for roast mountain sheep and hardtack, then held evening sick call. A wheezing sergeant was first in line. James thumped his chest and listened to the man's labored breathing with his stethoscope.

"Consumption, advanced," he told Sergeant Riley. "A portion of one lung is solidified. I don't know how you've come this far."

"Have to set an example for the men, can't run to sick call for every little thing."

James scowled. "From here on, you ride in the ambulance."

Two constipations, an ague, a cough and three headaches later, there was one man left in line, Private Frederick Lepper of Company L. He held out his right hand, which was wrapped in a dirty, blood-stained bandanna that stunk of infection. The steward unwound it, revealing a pus-swollen gash surrounded by angry red skin.

"Fell off my horse, sir, cut it on a sharp rock. Thought it'd get better on its own," Lepper said. "This mornin' when I got up, it was so swolled an' hurt so bad I couldn't move my fingers."

James told the steward to take Lepper inside the ambulance and give him two shot glasses of whiskey. The private gritted his teeth while James lanced, drained and cleaned the wound with carbolic acid. He told the steward to paint it with iodine and dress it, and then went back to his tent to write Fannie about the miserable day and sick call:

I often think, why live such a life as this. But perhaps "the sun may be shining tomorrow." Hope of the future is what keeps heavy hearts in this world of hardships. Well darling, I have until we get to the Yellowstone to finish this, so I will wait until the sun shines in my soul as well as from the heavens. I do so hope you are well again darling. I can hardly wait till I get another letter.

Snow frosted the wind-swept hilltops their first day on the move again, but by late morning, it was *hot as hell.*

Not long after noon, another messenger from Major General John Gibbon reported that his men were still camped on the north bank of the Yellowstone River opposite Rosebud Creek. There were a lot of Indians in the area and Gibbon needed reinforcements. Two privates and a teamster out hunting had been killed. One private was found with a head full of lead and two knives buried in his skull; the other's skull was bashed in. The teamster took a shot behind the ear. The Indians bashed his skull in and chopped it up with a hatchet.

"They seem content to take a scalp and steal a horse when the opportunity arises and don't seem interested in a real fight," the messenger said.

The expedition continued west in heat so intense, several men fainted and fell from their horses. James had a painful boil on his cheek; his ears and nose were aflame, he had a splitting headache, and his lips were so burned, it hurt to eat or talk.

A long line of men waited at evening sick call with sunburn, heat stroke, dehydration and fatigue. He rationed his limited supplies of ointments and headache powders and told them to drink plenty of water.

James wrote Fannie about Gibbon and the Indians: *I suppose when you get this we will be most ready to turn back. Hoping so, darling.*

They passed signs of a large buffalo herd in a hot, blasting wind the next day. Custer's hunting party killed deer in cottonwoods by a dry creek. Charley Reynolds bagged an old bull buffalo resting under a tree. James learned while eating venison and tough buffalo steak that pickets had spotted an Indian near camp.

The wind shifted from south to north overnight, bringing a bone-chilling mist. Terry and Custer and half a dozen scouts sat their mounts just ahead of the column.

"Safest course would be down O'Fallon Creek and up the Yellowstone to the mouth of the Powder," James heard Lonesome Charley Reynolds say.

Terry looked at Custer.

"Safest for scouts who can't find good ways through badlands," Custer said. "The shortest way's straight across to the Powder."

Reynolds' easy manner didn't change. "The badlands near the Powder can be treacherous. If this mist turns to rain, the wagons could mire. Be safer going down O'Fallon Creek."

"Makes sense, don't you think?" Terry asked Custer.

"Rain would be trouble either way. We can beat it by going straight across. I've got an instinct for these things, what I call bump of locality."

"How far?" Terry asked.

"Eighteen, maybe twenty miles," Custer replied.

Terry nodded, and Custer turned to Reno. "Major, you have command of the column! Follow my trail!"

They traveled over easy ground all morning. Around noon, they rode through rolling hills littered with buffalo carcasses. Some animals had been skinned and stripped of meat; many had been left to rot.

"They know we're coming and don't want to leave us any game," Calhoun said as they surveyed the awesome killing field.

Reno kept to ridgelines until he had no choice but to descend into a wet, sandy flat. Wagons mired and it took several hours to get them all through.

While they were waiting, James and Porter rode up a narrow ravine to its source, where James pointed toward a splash of green and purple. "Heliotrope," he said, pulling his horse close enough to touch the wet leaves and pluck a blossom. "We had these flowers in Oregon. My wife enjoyed them."

Custer was conferring with Terry and Reno when they returned. He'd found a pass through the badlands down to the Powder.

"Lead the way. Show us your 'bump of locality,'" Terry said.

The trail was soggy and some of the turns so narrow and tight, they had to unhitch the lead mules to get the wagons through.

"We get a good rain and the ravines will turn to gushers," Terry said.

Custer laughed. "General, you fret too much."

"Your bump of weather?" Terry asked.

The bitter wind calmed and the trail grew easier as they neared the valley. It was eight o'clock when they stopped on a flat above the river.

"Fifteen butt-bruising hours," James groaned to Porter, getting off his horse. "My legs are so stiff and my bones ache so much, I'm not sure I can walk."

He wrote Fannie: *Today for dinner we had beans, bacon, biscuit and butter, hardtack, coffee and an apple pudding and peas. . . . Of course we had some ashes and dirt but things tasted good and my appetite has not failed me once. . . .*

I am now somewhat inclined to think our stay up here will be short. We have not seen an Indian yet nor much signs & every one of the Command except a few think we will not find them on fighting terms. If there is a fight, he added, he'd wear his memento from her: *I have had my washing done today and had your blue necktie washed. It looks nice. . . . Love and kisses darling. From your loving Hub, J.M.D.*

15

Long, long ago, when the world was young and people had not come out yet, no flowers bloomed on the prairie. . . . Earth felt very sad because her robe lacked brightness and beauty. . . .A sweet little pink flower heard Earth's sad talking. "Do not be sad, Mother Earth. I will go upon your robe and beautify it."

—Lakota (Sioux): The Origin of the Prairie Rose

At least once a week, Fannie sat down in her parlor and reread all of James's letters, from the first written on the trail between Totten and Seward to his most recent one. Reviewing his experiences, and tracing his journey on the adjutant's maps, brought her closer to him. She knew each letter by heart and knew every letter's sequence. Still, she never tired of reading them.

She opened his second-to-last letter, written in camp on the Powder River on June 10:

We—our wing is going up the Powder River on a scout. The balance of Comd & wagons are going down to boats then up the Yellowstone or that is the current report. We are going to take pack mules and expect to be able to travel rapidly, but it has rained since yesterday &

not very rapidly will we go I guess for a day or two at least. I am well and am glad to think we are about to turn the home corner for I expect after this scout we will know when to expect to return. All in a hurry today so bye bye darling, love & kisses from your ever loving Husband.

One letter remained. Headed *Yellowstone, Mouth of Rosebud Creek, June 21ˢᵗ 76*, it was long and detailed and included a description of his scout with Reno's wing along with a token of his love—a pink rose blossom pressed between the pages.

She cupped the blossom in her hands, savored its fading scent and skipped ahead to two sentences near the end: *Rosebud Creek takes its name by being profusely bordered by the wild Roses like those of Warner. I send you one in this letter.*

She went to the dining room table, still covered with maps. What was it like riding through hostile Indian country? How did he feel? Was he tense or apprehensive? Knowing James, she didn't think so. He probably worried more about her being worried about him. Was he holding anything back? She knew he might, to "protect" her.

His wing's long scout covered two hundred eighty-five miles and took ten days. She knew that from his last letter. She traced his route—south up the Powder River, west to the Tongue, down the Tongue eight miles and then twenty-five miles west to Rosebud Creek, where he cut her rose blossom. They rode up Rosebud Creek twelve miles and then back down to its junction with the Yellowstone. From there, they traveled thirty-three miles down the Yellowstone and rejoined Custer and the six companies with him near the mouth of the Tongue. General Terry and his staff were nearby, too, on the "Far West" steamer, and Gibbon's forces were still camped at the mouth of the Rosebud. No one had heard anything from General George Crook, who was expected at any time with his force from Wyoming. *We found no Indians, not one, all old trails. They seem to be moving west and are driving the buffalo. I think it is very clear that we shall not see an Indian this summer.*

Fannie wiped her eyes with a hankie and thought once more: Could she believe him? Was he telling her everything? She hoped so.

His letter said they were preparing for one last scout with

Custer in command of all twelve Seventh Cavalry companies. They would ride up Rosebud Creek, west over to the Bighorn River and then down the Bighorn to the Yellowstone. She traced the route, again, and noted that their ride from Rosebud Creek to the Bighorn would take them across another river called the Little Bighorn.

Darling I did so hope I should hear from you on returning to the boat and may before we start out. . . . I fear we shall not find even a sign that is new this time. It is believed that the Indians have scattered and gone back to their reservations.

They hadn't encountered any Indians, and probably wouldn't; that was the important thing, as far as Fannie was concerned. James would be with all twelve cavalry companies under Custer's command. He would be safe.

I do so hope you are well again. I am very anxious to hear how you are getting along. I hope when we return from this scout we shall be nearly ready to return. Then darling only think we will have 300 or 400 miles to march home again. . . . Well darling I must close this as the boat goes down the river some little distance and the mail closes tonight and I want to be sure this goes in this mail.

Love & kisses darling, from your loving Hub, J.M. DeWolf

* * *

Reduced to skin and bones, John Mitzdorf spent his final weeks sleeping most of the time. More often than not, Fannie was by his side. When she wasn't, the fort's military wives, the hospital matron, laundresses and servants helped her keep vigil, sponging his sores and spooning water and broth into his dry mouth.

Every now and then, he opened his eyes and, real or imagined, Fannie and the others detected a smile.

Fannie was with him when he died on a sweltering night not long before the nation's Centennial. She'd nodded off and when she woke up and touched his hand, she knew he was gone. She thought his death would bring relief, but she only felt empty. "Your suffering is over," she whispered.

No one knew much about Mitzdorf, not even Fannie, only that

he'd come alone to America from Germany. Like many young men who made the Atlantic voyage during and after the war, he decided to get his start in the Army.

Fannie asked him several times about his family and what town he was from. He didn't want to talk about it, except to say he missed his mother's cooking. What's your mother's name? Fannie asked once. He pretended not to understand. She didn't ask again.

A military funeral for Private John Mitzdorf, Seventh Cavalry, date and place of birth unknown, was held on a blazing summer day in the middle of the parade ground with all of Totten's soldiers formed in dress uniforms around his flag-draped wooden casket. He was buried in Fort Totten's cemetery.

After the burial, Fannie sat quietly with her eyes closed in her favorite parlor chair. Finally she picked up pen and paper and wrote James about Mitzdorf's death, the ceremony and burial, knowing he wouldn't get the letter until after his last scout. Placing it on the end table, she went outside to the porch, where she sat in a rocking chair with James's last letter open in her lap. The dried pink rose blossom fell at her feet. Picking it up, she pressed it to her nose. Its sweet scent had faded away. She looked down at James's words on the paper. Would they fade away, too? Would their meaning fade? She needed to feel him, to smell him, to taste him, to see his face and know with certainty the meaning of every word. Skimming quickly, she searched for reassuring clues—not the passage about the rose, not his declarations of love; she knew James loved her. Was he telling her everything? Was she missing something? Was he holding back because he loved her? That's what she needed to know. He would ride with the Seventh Cavalry on one last scout. And then they would start home. Most men thought the Indians had already departed for their reservations.

Reassured, she sighed, placed the blossom back in its letter and placed all of the letters back into her trunk. For a long time, she lay awake in bed with her hands on her stomach, reciting prayers for James's safe return.

Finally, she drifted off to sleep.

16

33 miles, continued up the Rosebud C, find large deserted camps, the valley completely barren. Has been an enormous number of horses passed about 10 to 20 days ago, 11 miles above where Reno was on the 17th, very hot. . . . Marched 10 miles and found a large (Indian trail) branch nearly as large as main stream, found another 7 miles beyond, marched within a few miles of the forks, found lots of new signs, old camps in profusion.
—*James DeWolf Diary entries, June 23–24, 1876*

Mounted behind Custer with Reno's staff, James looked down the long column—an impressive force of over 650 mounted men on horses sorted by color—sorrels, bays, grays, blacks and one company on mixed colors. Bugles blared and cavalrymen urged their horses to a brisk trot. James relished the spectacle and then turned his attention to Custer in his clean buckskins, sporting a long red tie and light gray campaign hat.

The last company thundered by and Custer spurred his thoroughbred Vic through the dust up to Terry and Gibbon. Horse prancing, he saluted and swept his hat with a flourish. As he turned his horse to leave, Gibbon yelled, "Custer! Don't be greedy! Wait for us! There are Indians enough for all of us!"

Custer laughed and urged Vic at a gallop toward the head of the formation.

Not far up the Rosebud, he halted the column and gave his marching orders: "There will be no wing commanders! I will command all! Major Reno, you and your staff will ride at the head with me and my staff! Captain Benteen will take rear guard!"

They halted again about 4 p.m., and after supper, Custer held officers' call near the gurgling stream.

"Gentlemen, you're probably wondering why I left the Gatling gun behind. You may also wonder why I rejected an offer to take extra cavalry companies from Gibbon's command." Custer paused, seemingly waiting for a response.

"You all know the Gatling taken on Major Reno's scout slowed his battalion. Worse yet, three men were seriously injured when the gun overturned. With artillery, we could fall behind and arrive too late to meet Terry and Gibbon at the hostiles' camp."

"That's all well and good general. But I, for one, am sorry you didn't take the extra cavalry companies. I think we will regret not having them," said Benteen.

"I thank you for your view, Captain Benteen, but I decided and Generals Terry and Gibbon agreed that it would be better to leave all of those companies with them. The Seventh is the finest fighting unit west of the Mississippi. We have no equals, gentlemen. We will travel better and fight more cohesively without the Second Cavalry."

Custer looked at the ground and then stared at his officers for several moments. He rambled about defensive plans in the event of an attack and covered details related to their marching formation. Several times, he stopped and asked if anyone had any comments or suggestions. No one spoke up. Finally, he said he was aware that several officers had been critical of decisions he'd made during their march from Fort Lincoln.

"Some of you have even taken complaints outside our regiment, to General Terry's staff. This I will not tolerate." His upper lip twitched under his mustache and his face flushed. "If you have *any* recommendations, make them through proper channels. Anyone who makes their views known in any other way will face serious discipline."

Walking away, James overheard one officer say to another: "General Custer must think he's going to be killed."

"Why do you say that?" the other asked.

"Just the way he was back there, he never asks for advice or explains himself."

Soft singing wafted from the direction of Custer's campsite after sunset.

"Our leader's favorites are trying to cheer him with a serenade," McDougall said.

"God rest his soul," James replied.

"That's a funeral line, Doc." Benny Hodgson looked surprised.

"I only meant," James started. "I don't know what I meant."

It was blazing hot when they reached the first abandoned Indian camp the next day. The trail left by the Indians cut a wide swath from the valley's western hills to the rock outcroppings on the eastern edge. Every blade of grass had been cropped or trampled, and the bare dirt was pocked by thousands of human footprints and pony tracks, and scarred by deep ruts left by travois.

"I'll be goddamned," a scout said, spitting a stream of tobacco.

Most cavalrymen were dumbstruck, but not the Indian scouts. Several chattered and gesticulated excitedly as they rode ahead, guiding their horses back and forth from one side of the valley to the other. One made a slashing motion across his neck. Bloody Knife rode just ahead of James near Custer, muttering to several other Arikara scouts, who grew even more agitated.

"He says half the Sioux nation is here," an interpreter told Custer.

Custer rode ahead alone and walked his horse in a wide circle, examining the Sioux trail. Returning to the column, he declared, "We'll find them soon and punish them like we did on the Washita!"

"This won't be no Washita, general," a scout replied. "This is no small band of cold and starving Cheyenne."

That evening, James, Porter, Hodgson and McDougall sat together on a western hill above their valley camp with their backs against a large rock. Porter lit his pipe, and then Hodgson and McDougall lit theirs. The eastern bluffs glowed orange-red as the sun set behind them.

"Think I'll cut some more rosebuds," James said. "I cut the last on June sixteenth, my wife's birthday, and forgot to mention it in my letter."

"Hoping to get yourself back into her good graces, are you?" Hodgson chuckled.

"I'm always in her good graces." James smiled.

He cut three blossoms this time—I love you—and rejoined his comrades. They watched the bluffs on the other side of the valley fade to black, each lost in his own reveries.

● ◯ ● ◯ ●

The abandoned camps increased as they continued up the Rosebud on June 24, until there were *old camps in profusion*, as James wrote in his diary that day. Near one of the camps, Indian scouts gathered around a rock with a pictograph showing two mortally wounded buffalo, one shot, the other one speared.

"They say the Sioux left it as a warning," an interpreter told Custer. "The drawing's ancient, but they're too worked up to see that."

Farther on, they found a soldier's scalp on a stick planted with his hat in the middle of the trail. "Probably from one of Crook's men, they must've already had a fight with the Indians," a scout said.

A little farther up the trail, they found a huge Sun Dance ground with a towering pole in the middle of a circle of beaten-down earth. A mound of dirt was piled around its base and it was topped by a buffalo skull with grass stuffed into its eye and nose cavities. The dance area was circled by an eight-foot high branch wall, open in the central dance area and covered around the perimeter with branches and hides.

"Never seen a dance lodge anywhere near this big, and that pole's twice as tall as any I've seen," the scout Isaiah Dorman said, shaking his head.

"They held war dances here?" James asked.

"Nah, their annual Sun Dance, dances for visions, could be they saw a great victory in battle, or maybe a successful buffalo hunt and fat times," Dorman replied.

Several men rummaged through feathers, eagle bone whistles, beaded headbands, containers with tobacco and other offerings around the base of the pole.

"Look, redskin jerky!" A private held his trophy high. It looked like a black stick or roll of smoked meat, tapered at one end, about eight inches long.

Dorman laughed. "It's a fertility offering, private! You could call it jerky, but I expect you won't want to eat it. It's a dried buffalo's cock. They leave it at the base of the pole to assure the dancers' virility."

Everyone roared as the private tossed the penis like a red-hot poker.

"There's a drawing in the dirt over there," Charley Reynolds said, pointing toward a sweat lodge where Crow and white scouts were gathered with several soldiers. "The Crows are worked up. They say it shows attacking Indians and dying soldiers."

James and several others joined the excited Crows and other spectators around a pile of rocks at the end of a row of buffalo skulls. On top of the pile, a large bull's skull faced the back of a cow's skull. Sticks sharpened at one end pointed from the large skull to the smaller one. "They say the skulls mean the Sioux will fight like bulls and soldiers will run and die like cows."

Custer turned angry red. "Destroy it! Destroy everything!"

Shouting and whooping, soldiers and Indian scouts crashed their horses through sweat lodges and over buffalo skulls. Men tied ropes to the arbor's poles and pulled it down with their horses, then tried for some time to topple the Sun Dance pole.

It wouldn't budge.

17

The opposite hill was equally steep and dangerous, but the soldiers scrambled up in a most unwarlike manner. Here some of the privates showed fine presence of mind and uncommon bravery. One of the officers of the fleeing command aroused the highest admiration of the Indians. He emptied his revolver in a most effective way, and had crossed the river, when a gunshot brought him down. There were three noted young warriors of three different lodges . . . vying with one another for bravery. They all happened to pursue this officer; each one was intent upon knocking him off with a war-club before the others, but the officer dispatched every one of them. The Indians told me of finding peculiar instruments on his person, from which I thought it likely this brave man was Dr. DeWolf, who was killed there.

—Account of the June 25 Battle of the Little Bighorn written by Doctor Charles Alexander Eastman, "Ohiyesa" (Winner), Eastern-educated, Dakota Indian and government physician at Pine Ridge Agency, S.D., based on interviews with Indians who took part in the fight

They stopped the night of June 24 where the Indian trail turned west toward the Little Bighorn. James led his horse to the cold, clear Rosebud, where green willows and pink roses flourished. Exhausted, he looked up and down the long line of horses, mules and men by the stream, and felt all alone. They were on the trail of a huge band of hostile Indians who'd held a big dance after an apparent victory over General Crook and his men. The Indians had left scalps along the trail as a warning. But James wasn't afraid; he didn't fear death. He might never see Fannie again. That's what he feared. He wanted to tell her he was sorry—for not even listening when she said he could leave the Army and stay in Boston, for telling her he intended to stay in Dakota for another year, whether she liked it or not, for nagging her to get a female companion and to keep her door locked at night, for his jealousy and insecurity. For what he wanted to tell her now: "Fannie, I love you, I'm sorry for how I've been."

He tethered his horse and joined the other officers for hardtack, salt pork and beans. Some men were withdrawn, others chatty. He'd seen it during the war. The prospect of a bloody fight affected men differently.

McDougall pointed toward a fire where men had gathered around Charley Reynolds. The quiet, blue-eyed veteran had laid clothing on the ground and was taking more things out of his saddlebags.

"Holy mother of Jesus," someone said, "he's giving everything away."

Reynolds held a shirt up. Several men shook their heads and walked away. Most stayed, too embarrassed to turn their backs on the respected scout. One man took a shirt, another a comb. Reynolds gave away a jacket, buckskin pants and a beaded belt.

"Enough of yer damned nonsense, Charley!" A scout refused a fur hat and paced away. Everyone scattered, leaving Reynolds alone.

Even the chatty officers were quiet now. Finally, Benteen said, "See here, fellows, if I were you, I'd be getting as much sleep as you can, and getting it soon. I've got a feeling we'll be up before long, for an all-night march."

Benteen was right. James had just closed his eyes when Custer's adjutant announced that all officers should report to the commanding officer at once. James looked at his watch, almost 10 p.m. He made it to officers' call just in time to hear they would depart in one hour and move as close as possible to the divide between the Rosebud and Little Bighorn before daylight.

James rode at the head of Reno's companies just behind Custer and his staff. It was pitch dark and overcast, so everyone stayed in line by following the noise ahead—heavy hooves on hard ground, and clanking canteens, pots, weapons and other gear. Noise carried so well that James could hear the brays of pack mules at the rear.

"Some stealthy approach," he said to Porter.

They halted around 2 a.m. near several small ponds, but the water was so alkaline, the thirsty horses and mules refused to drink. Some men napped. Many smoked and chatted about what might happen in the next day or two. James, Hodgson and Porter fed their horses and reclined on a flat rock. Faint stars flickered through thinning clouds. Heat lightening flashed and rippled overhead.

"Can white men have visions?" Hodgson asked.

"Why do you ask, Benny?" James replied.

"It came to me that if I'm shot off my horse, or my horse is shot from under me, I'll grab the stirrup of another horse so I can be dragged to safety."

"If you're unhorsed and I'm nearby, jump up behind me." James smiled. "It'll be more comfortable than bouncing along the prairie."

They moved out before dawn and climbed toward the divide between the Rosebud and Little Bighorn. The sun rose pale pink, deepened to peach orange and blazed white-hot by the time they settled in a depression surrounded by hills a few miles from the divide.

James was resting with his hat over his face when Hodgson shook him. "Custer's been to a lookout at the top. He couldn't see anything through the haze, but the Crow scouts assured him there's a large village stretching for miles on the west bank of the river. The Crows say the Indians aren't packing to leave, so it looks like we'll stay here today and most of the night and then position ourselves for a pre-dawn attack."

Moments later, someone shouted, "General, the redskins know we're here! A pack was discovered missing from a mule and when soldiers went back to get it, they caught three braves going through it. They killed one but the others ran into the hills, toward the divide!"

Custer's face clouded. "We move at once!"

A short time later, Custer's adjutant, First Lieutenant William Cooke, relayed their marching orders: McDougall would take men to the rear for pack train guard duty. Benteen would lead three companies on a scout to the southwest to look for fleeing Indians, and then head back north toward the Indian camp. Reno's three companies and five led by Custer would follow a dry creek bed directly down to the river.

James removed his sweat-soaked yellow bandanna, wiped his face with it, stuffed it into a saddlebag and pulled out his clean navy blue scarf.

"The tie from your wife?" Porter asked.

"I promised her I'd wear it in battle, my good luck."

Riding through rough hills on the south bank of the dry creek, Reno's wing fell behind Custer's companies, which outpaced them on the north bank's easier ground. Not long after he lost sight of Custer's column, James heard Indian war cries ahead. Someone yelled, "The fight's begun!" But as they rounded a hill, all they saw below were Custer's waiting companies and whooping Arikara scouts staging a mock attack against a lone painted tepee.

Custer waved to Reno to bring his companies over to the north side of the creek, and as they approached, James saw that the slashed-open tepee was empty except for an Indian brave laid out on a decorated burial platform.

"Injuns, general! There they go, runnin' like devils!" a scout yelled, pointing downhill from the tepee. "Must be that dead brave's mourners, forty or fifty of 'em, hell bent for leather toward the Injun camp!"

The bugler signaled the unfurling of the battle flag. Custer snapped orders and Cooke rode toward Reno's column. "Major Reno! The general orders you to take your companies along with the Ree scouts down this creek and charge the hostiles! The Arikaras will capture the Sioux ponies while you charge the camp!"

"The general will support me?"

"Yes, major!"

Reno started back to his column, and Custer spurred his horse to catch him. It appeared to James that while Reno attacked the south end of the camp, Custer planned to take his companies north down the east side of the river and then cross over to attack the camp's flank.

◇ ◇ ◇ ◇

The very earth seemed to grow Indians and they were running towards me.

—Major Marcus A. Reno

They rode down the dry creek two abreast, and as Reno led his battalion into the river, Cooke caught up and shouted: "Major! General Custer wants to make his orders clear! Charge the village! You will be supported by the whole outfit!"

"Custer will support me?"

"Yes!"

Reno let his men water their horses and then gathered them behind timber to organize the attack. While the Indian scouts went after the hostiles' ponies, the cavalrymen would ride four abreast and then spread to a skirmish line at the sound of the bugle.

Conspicuous in his white straw hat, Reno rode well ahead, picking up the pace from a trot to a lope and then a gallop when he saw a dozen braves fleeing ahead of him. The bugler sounded the charge. The big horses thundered down the valley, and the cavalry spread into a long blue line.

The warriors disappeared around a tree-lined bend. James glanced to his left. The Indian scouts already were driving Sioux ponies up-river. The plan appeared to be working. As they rounded the timber, he saw a warrior on a brown and white paint with his hand raised in a sign of peace. Carbines cracked along the cavalry line. The brave turned and appeared to yell and then turned back and fired at the advancing soldiers. More braves rode forward. Some took cover and fired from trees near the river.

Reno slowed to a trot and then reined his horse to a stop, shouting orders for commanders to dismount their men. They marched forward, firing their carbines into the village and at the braves in the trees. The Indians fell back. It appeared to James that they were engaged in a rear guard action to protect their fleeing women, elders and children. But in the blink of an eye, a dust cloud boiled between the soldiers and the village, and from the billows rode hundreds of screaming Indians, pouring a heavy fire.

"Where the hell is Custer?" Reno yelled. "Where's Benteen?"

The soldiers advanced, but hundreds of more braves joined the counter-attack.

"Take the horses into the timber!" Reno looked toward James. "Doctors DeWolf and Porter, withdraw to the timber and prepare for wounded!"

James and Porter dashed into the timber, followed closely by Reno and then by retreating soldiers, who established a defensive line in the trees. A soldier's horse bolted toward the village and was swallowed by the dust. A sergeant fell on the prairie, trampled by pony hooves and riddled with bullets and arrows. A private panicked, broke from the defensive line and dashed for the river.

"Stop him!" Reno shouted. "No man leaves the line without my order!"

James watched in horror as a Crow scout chased the man down, bashed his head with a club and slit his throat. Across the river, dust billowed from behind the high hills. James imagined Custer's five companies galloping to their aid, led by the general at the fore with his red tie flying.

Heavy fire around him broke the spell, and Reno yelled, "Mount!"

Soldiers scrambled for their horses. Almost immediately, one mounted soldier was shot in the neck. In the same instant, a bullet struck Bloody Knife in the head, splattering the Ree scout's blood, skull fragments and brains on Reno's face. As Bloody Knife hit the ground, Sergeant John Ryan yelled, "Private Lorentz is hit!" Blood gushing from his neck, Lorentz rolled off his horse.

James jumped to the ground and rushed to his aid, jerking his horse along by its reins. "Roll him on his side! He's drowning in blood!"

Ryan and another man rolled Lorentz over. The fatal bullet spewed from his mouth in a torrent of blood. Lorentz was dead before James could do anything.

"Dismount!" Reno wiped gore from his face with a large, white handkerchief, pushed his hair back, tied the bloody cloth around his head and then countermanded his order. "Mount and charge! Back toward the ford!"

Few heard Reno's orders in the din of gunfire, war cries and the screams of terrified horses, but most took the cue when they saw soldiers near Reno mount and run south. James jumped on his horse and followed but stopped to help Porter, who was on his knees near the south edge of the timber beside a fallen soldier.

Porter looked up. "Get out of here James! This man's a goner!"

James dismounted and dropped beside Porter, smelling odors from the soldier's vacated bladder and bowels. Warriors, bent low on their ponies, dashed by not more than ten yards away, pursuing fleeing soldiers. Bullets ripped through leaves above their heads, but the warriors were too intent on the chase to bother with Porter and James. The fallen man was rapidly fading from loss of blood.

"I bandaged his wound!" Porter yelled. "There's nothing more we can do!"

The terrified soldier pleaded, "For God's sake, doc, don't leave me to be tortured by those fiends! Shoot me!"

"You'll be gone in a minute," Porter told the man in a kindly voice.

James uncorked his whiskey bottle and held it to the man's lips.

"Now get the hell out of here James! I'm right behind you!" Porter yelled.

They mounted and urged their horses out of the timber. Three warriors went after James, vying for coup honors and the kill.

Pistol in hand, James shot one from his horse at point-blank range as the brave raised his club. Another Indian caught up and James fired again. The young brave looked startled as he toppled from his horse. The third, approaching James from behind on the other side, swung his club. James felt rushing air as it grazed his ear. He turned, fired and missed. The brave drew closer with his club raised. James fired again and the young warrior fell.

Dead and wounded horses and men littered their path as James and Porter neared the river. Blood-red water churned with the last of the cavalry trying to cross. James's horse plunged off the high cut bank into the cold water with Porter's just behind as hundreds of braves circled and fired from their ponies, more intent on showing their riding skills than on taking careful aim at fleeing soldiers.

Scrambling up the muddy bank, James's horse veered left. Porter's horse dashed past him to the right toward a wide ravine where Reno and most of his men frantically scrambled for safety. A few men had stayed behind and were crouched at the foot of the hills, providing covering fire.

James was about to turn right and follow Porter when he saw Hodgson face-down on the ground. He reined his horse. "Benny!"

"Dead, sir! Shot off his horse on the opposite bank! Fell into the river, come up, grabbed a stirrup strap and got pulled across! Shot dead after he crawled up the bank!"

James recognized the soldier yelling at him. It was Private Elihu Clear, his orderly, who was one of the soldiers providing covering fire. He ignored Clear, jumped off his horse and crouched by Hodgson. "Benny!" He grabbed his friend's shoulder and turned him onto his back.

Clear, on one knee, held his horse's reins with one hand and fired his pistol with the other. Bullets kicked dust around him. "C'mon, sir! Look down there!" he yelled, pointing downstream.

"They're crossing the river, be here soon!"

James looked up at Clear just as the soldier's body snapped in a spray of blood. "I'm hit!" Clear holstered his weapon, jerked his horse by the reins, found a stirrup and swung a leg over the saddle. The terrified animal bolted, carrying Clear up a narrow ravine. James glanced upstream, where cavalrymen scrambled to safety, then jumped on his horse and rode after his wounded striker.

○ ○ ○ ○

The ravines east of the Little Bighorn reached like spread fingers into the hills. The wide one to the right took Reno, Porter and the others to the southeast, away from the Indians advancing from the north. A high ridge shielded their climb. The narrow ravine Clear and James rode up took them northeast toward the Indians. It was steep and shallow, offering no cover. Some of the pursuing warriors rode directly up-river along the east bank while others climbed the hills and advanced along the top of the bluffs, laying a heavy fire from above while their comrades advanced from below.

Clear's horse plunged up the brush-choked ravine, kicking dust in James's face. When the going became too steep for his horse, he jumped and scrambled in a desperate attempt to get out of the ravine, over a ridge and down to cover on the other side. He was near the top with James not far behind when a Cheyenne brave aimed carefully and brought him down. James ignored bullets hitting the dirt around him and knelt beside the mortally wounded soldier. As he took bandages from his medical bag, he heard frantic soldiers yelling at him to get away.

"It's too late for me, Doc." Clear gasped in pain. "Save yourself." He coughed up blood and added, "Now I won't see that squaw's face no more."

James looked up toward the frantic shouting and saw a dozen soldiers on top of a high ridge to his south, gesticulating and pointing their carbines toward the hill above him. "Doctor DeWolf! Get out of there!" Several knelt and fired, but the advancing Indians were out of their range.

James crouched beside Clear's body and reloaded his pistol, then stood to run. Above him, several Indians scrambled down the steep hill. Others advanced from below. He leveled his revolver and aimed at the closest brave descending from above. Before he could fire, he felt a burning sensation, dropped his gun and fell to his knees. A red stain spread over his pale blue shirt.

He grabbed his pistol and scrambled toward the top of the ravine's south ridge. A few more steps and he'd roll to safety down the other side. His head was light. He fell to his knees at the end of the ridge and tried to raise his revolver. It fell from his hand. He looked down to pick it up and saw moccasins. A dark hand grabbed his weapon. He looked up into a painted face contorted with hate and a blood-curdling cry.

His own pistol's muzzle flashed before his eyes.

◼ ◆ ◼

After a day of fierce fighting on June 26, the Indians broke camp. A long, wide procession—thousands of Sioux and Cheyenne—headed south up the Little Bighorn toward the Bighorn Mountains. Shortly after sunset, Porter organized a recovery detail and headed down to the river, where he told his hospital steward, "See to the men down here. I'll take four men up to the point where Doctor DeWolf and his striker fell."

Porter found Clear's body on the side of a ridge. James was at the top, not more than ten yards away, sprawled on his back. Swarming flies feasted on his head and torso. Porter dropped to his knees and angrily swatted with his hat. The front of James's shirt was stained brown-red from just below his sternum to his belt; blood stained his pants in a semi-circle below.

Porter sighed and rubbed his eyes. James's face was gone, and his body was already ripe from the heat. Porter turned away and fell to all fours. Dry heaves racked his body. He took several deep breaths, regained his composure, and turned back to James. "Farewell, dear friend," he said, resting a hand gently on James' shoulder.

Porter searched James' pockets. He found and removed his

diaries, remarkably unstained, and then used a surgical knife to cut a lock of hair from his partially scalped head. "I will make sure your wife gets your things, your diaries and a lock of your hair. I know you loved her dearly, and she you."

They wrapped James in a tent fly, scraped a shallow grave and were throwing dirt on his body when shouts came from below.

"Doctor Porter! Hostiles are coming across the river!"

"We're coming!" Porter yelled, and then told the soldiers, "Go ahead."

He placed the lock of hair and James's diaries in his medical bag and threw a few more handfuls of dirt onto the body. Hearing gunfire and war whoops, he scrambled down the hill. The Indians fired a few wild shots, and then rode away. Porter and the others scrambled back up the wide ravine.

● ● ●

On the morning of June 27, 1876, Porter returned to the place where James fell and supervised a more complete burial, fortifying the mound with rocks. He marked the grave with a stake driven completely into the ground, then wrote James's name on a slip of paper, stuffed it into an empty cartridge shell, and drove the shell into the top of the stake. His post-mortem examination found that Doctor James Madison DeWolf, U.S. Army Acting Assistant Surgeon, had been shot once in the stomach and six times in the face and head.

18

July 11, 1876 - Today about noon received intelligence of the unfortunate disaster that befell our troops under the command of General Custer on the Little Big Horn River.

Four of the Companies of the 7th Cavalry engaged in this fight viz "E," "D," "I" & "L" were well known to this post they having formed part of the garrison of the post at different times. Among the officers killed, Captain [Myles] Keogh, Liet. [James] Porter, and Act. Asst. Surgeon James M. DeWolf U.S.A. were known to everyone here and their loss is deeply regretted by all, as they were universally respected and liked.

If the report proves true this will leave four widows at the post as a result of this engagement—viz—Mrs. Dr. DeWolf, Mrs. Crisfield laundry of L Co., Mrs. Hohmeyer and four children and Mrs. McElroy of "E" Company 7th Cavalry.

—Entry by Doctor James Ferguson, Post Surgeon, in Fort Totten's Medical History Log

Fannie lit her bedside lamp and marked an X over July 3. James and the Seventh Cavalry should have finished their last scout and would be Dakota-bound soon. His last letter, written June 21 at the mouth of Rosebud Creek, said: *I hope when we return from this scout we shall be nearly ready to return. Then* *darling only think we will have 300 or 400 miles to march home again.*

Home again.

She imagined they might celebrate the Centennial at their Yellowstone base camp. James would bathe in the icy river and enjoy an Independence Day feast, maybe roast antelope, his favorite, with biscuits and beans, and a double helping of peach or cherry cobbler. He would write another long letter about the cavalry's scout, and many more letters during their return. He should be back sometime in August. She would agree to another year in Dakota, and they would talk about their future. She might tell him about her miscarriage. Could she ever tell him? She didn't know. She fussed around their quarters. Everything would be perfect the day he returned, including the pink rose blossom placed on the calendar by their bed.

After her noon meal, she walked with Edna to the Hunts' quarters, where the women worked on their handwork in stifling heat. Fannie's needles clacked through rows of a sweater for James and then fell silent. She slipped the needle out of the last row.

"Tearing it up again?" Edna asked.

"The sleeves still don't match the front. I don't know why I chose such a complicated pattern." She rolled the unraveled black yarn into a ball, wiped her brow and stretched her arms, airing circles of perspiration on her pale blue gingham dress.

"It will be beautiful when it's finished," Edna said. "Your husband will love it."

They worked in heat and silence until the servant girl answered a knock at the door. "It's Missus McLaughlin, Mum. She'd like to see you."

"Tell her to come in," Missus Hunt responded.

"She said she'd wait at the door."

Fannie glanced up and then wondered what was wrong when the fort commander's wife and Marie spoke in hushed tones in the entry. She felt a sick feeling in the pit of her stomach when the two women entered the parlor. Her heart sank when her eyes locked with Marie's and her friend looked away.

"The Indians here believe they know something about our

cavalry companies in Montana," Missus Hunt said with a grim look.

Fannie's stomach knotted. She dropped the ball of yarn, which unwound across the floor. Marie started for it, stopped, looked at Fannie and nervously cleared her throat.

"For the past couple days, the Indians have been behaving strangely. My closest Dakota friends wouldn't speak to me, or even make eye contact." Marie glanced at Fannie and looked away. "I told my husband there was something wrong when he arrived from Jamestown yesterday. When he asked Chief Little Fish and the other leaders, they had nothing to say." Marie glanced at Fannie again and then quickly down at the floor. "When I pressed my good friend Wenonah again today, she told me there had been a terrible battle on the Little Bighorn River at a place the Indians call Greasy Grass. Many men of the Seventh Cavalry were killed."

Fannie gasped.

Edna touched Fannie's arm. "How could they know before us?"

"News travels fast among the plains Indians." Marie glanced at Fannie again. "My friend said the cavalry divided and attacked a huge Lakota and Cheyenne camp in two places several miles apart. All of the soldiers in one battle were killed. Most in the other battle survived."

"What about Doctor DeWolf?" Edna asked.

Marie sighed. "The Indians didn't know who they were fighting. They didn't even know Custer was there."

"So you don't know if General Custer was killed?"

Marie shook her head.

"Or Doctor DeWolf, or the husbands of other women at Totten?"

She shook her head.

Edna leaned close and whispered in Fannie's ear, "Stay with us until we know he's safe. You can sleep in Jimmie's room."

Fannie excused herself after supper, curled up in the small bed next to the crib and pulled the sheet over her head. She didn't stir when Edna came in and laid Jimmie down. She lay awake listening to the boy's soft sounds.

When he fussed, she picked him up and took him outside. Cradling him in her arms, she pushed softly in a wood slat rocking chair and gazed at the black sky. The stars and moon would be the same above James, wherever he was. She remembered her earlier foolish fears, but now she felt certain he was alive. He would never do anything foolhardy, would never be reckless.

◦ ◦ ◦ ◦ ◦

A mail carrier arrived on July 7 with news from the *Bismarck Tribune* that the Seventh Cavalry had indeed suffered a terrible defeat with hundreds killed. The story reaffirmed earlier accounts that Custer and all of the men with him had been killed while most of the men with Major Reno had survived. Fannie breathed a sigh of relief. James was in Reno's wing.

By the time she heard about the *Tribune* story, news of the Little Bighorn disaster had spread from the *Helena Herald* in Montana by wire to the Associated Press in Salt Lake City, and from there like wildfire on telegraph wires throughout the country. On July 6, the *New York Times* published several long articles about the battle, including one based on a special dispatch with detailed news about Reno's companies. An exhausted rider delivered the news to the adjutant at Fort Totten shortly after dawn on July 8.

General Hunt personally delivered the dispatches to Fannie immediately after reading them. "I wanted you to see the stories before the rumors start flying," he said, drawing her attention to details about Reno's fight:

While Custer attacked the huge Indian village in one location, she read, Reno *fell on them with three companies of cavalry, and was almost instantly surrounded, and after one hour or more of vigorous fighting, during which he lost Lieuts. Hodgson and McIntosh and Dr. DeWolf and twelve men . . .*

Fannie gasped and clapped a hand over her mouth.

"It's not official," Hunt said. "General Sherman has stated that he believes the accounts coming in are exaggerated. Even one of the *New York Times* stories says 'all is bustle and confusion' at headquarters in Chicago. Telegrams are coming in so fast that no one has had time to sort fact from fiction. They're keeping everything confidential until they've ascertained the true story. The plain truth is, we don't know Doctor DeWolf's status and won't know until we have the official report."

Fannie searched Hunt's eyes but knew he had nothing more. She took a deep breath, steeled herself, and continued reading. The dispatch said that in addition to James and the other two officers, twelve enlisted men and several Indian scouts were killed during Reno's fight in the valley. Many more were wounded before Reno *cut his way through to the river and gained a bluff 300 feet in height, where he entrenched and was soon joined by Col. Benson with four companies.*

"Benson" must be Captain Benteen, Fannie thought. If the report had his name wrong, it could have been wrong about James, too. She went to her quarters, prayed, and told herself the report about James couldn't be true. Most of Reno's men had survived. James must be one of them.

More dispatches arrived the next day. Some named Hodgson, McIntosh and James as among the men killed. Some didn't. General Hunt told Fannie the most recent reports listing her husband as among those killed were based on the earlier report. Editors simply took the information off the wire and repeated it. There was nothing new.

Fannie and the other officers' wives spent their days in the Hunts' parlor. They sang hymns, read bible verses, prayed, and watched for riders with news. In bed at night, Fannie recited silent prayers. The Twenty-third Psalm was her rod and her staff.

◆ ◆ ◆

But look! At the Officers Quarters is a group of excited women. . . . We are at Fort Totten and today's mail brings the news of the battle, the names of [those] killed.

—Account of the day wives at Fort Totten learned from the official report whose husbands were killed in the Little Bighorn battle, published in the June, 1913 issue of the "Fort Totten Review"

Fannie kept vigil in a chair by a front window in the Hunts' quarters, so she was the first to see the courier on July 11. While the other women continued singing, "Jesus loves me," she began a silent recitation of the Twenty-third Psalm and went outside. The others followed.

Across the parade ground, Mary Crisfield, wife of Private William Crisfield, stepped out from the laundry building, drenched in sweat. Mary Hohmeyer, wife of First Sergeant Frederick Hohmeyer, and Nora McElroy, wife of Trumpeter Thomas McElroy, joined her. A private left the adjutant's office and returned with the chaplain. The mail carrier came out, jumped on his pony and galloped off toward the reservation.

Ten minutes passed. "What could they be doing?" Fannie asked, rubbing perspiration from her eyes. Another forty-five minutes passed. The scout returned with Chief Little Fish, Arousing Hawk and another brave. Another twenty minutes passed before a sergeant walked up the boardwalk toward the enlisted wives. General Hunt and his adjutant walked across the parade ground to the Hunts' quarters.

"We have a dispatch addressed to the wives of Seventh Cavalry men stationed at Fort Totten." General Hunt looked at Fannie. "Your husband is the only officer Missus DeWolf." He handed her a sealed envelope. "The chaplain will hold a service in our quarters, and then, if you would please, you will open and read the dispatch for *all* the wives to hear."

Fannie took the envelope with a trembling hand.

○ ◇ ○

One of them carries the letter. They enter the house of the commanding officer. A few Indians are standing near. Chief Little Fish an onlooker. One woman attempts to open the letter, it falls to the floor. The surgeon's wife picks it up. She, who has often ministered to the wounded and dying, reads with a voice full of courage the name of an officer. A woman swoons. Another— a fainting cry. Another—I need not tell. . . .

Do you ask the names of these brave men? You will find them in granite on the field where they fell, a part of the cherished history of our country.

—*June 1913 issue of "Fort Totten Review"*

Thoughts raced through Fannie's head. Were all the married men from Totten killed? Only some? Was James alive? The other men with wives at Fort Totten were with Custer on that fateful day. James wasn't! How cruel to make them wait.

Edna put an arm around Fannie and led her into the Hunts' parlor, where ladder-back chairs had been quickly arranged for the service. Fannie sat in the middle of the first row. Her right hand held the envelope, resting on a hymnal in her lap. Her left hand clutched the gold cross necklace with rubies.

The Hunts sat on one side of her, the fort commander rigid with his eyes straight ahead, his wife with her head bowed and her lips moving in silent prayer. Doctor and Edna Ferguson sat on Fannie's other side. Edna brushed Fannie's hand with a reassuring touch. Fannie looked at her and then down at the envelope on the hymnal.

Post officers and wives filled the next row, in front of the enlisted men's wives and the McLaughlins. Little Fish, Arousing Hawk and the other brave stood in the back of the sweltering hot room.

"Let us pray." The chaplain recited the Lord's Prayer and followed with seemingly endless readings and hymns. How could he make them wait?

He put his hymnal down—and commenced a half-hour sermon, followed by the Twenty-third Psalm. Fannie whispered the words, adding her personal prayer. "Lord, I do want, I want James. Please God, let him be alive." And then near the end, "I do fear evil, God, please, erase my fears with joy."

"We have a dispatch addressed to the wives here whose husbands were in the battle on the Little Bighorn River. It includes the names of those men who have passed on to a better place." The chaplain spoke solemnly, bowed his head for a few moments and then looked directly at Fannie. "Missus DeWolf, please open and read the dispatch."

Hands shaking, she tried to open the envelope. It fell to the floor. Edna picked it up, put her arm around Fannie and whispered, "I'll read it. Be brave. You know your husband loves you dearly, and eternally."

Edna stood erect, removed the dispatch, took a deep breath and with a strong, clear voice read: "We regret to inform you that the following men of the Seventh Cavalry, whose wives are at Fort Totten, fell bravely fighting in the service of their country on the 25th day of June, 1876, during an engagement with hostile Indians in Montana Territory:"

She paused to regain her composure before reading the names of the dead.

"Acting Assistant Surgeon, Doctor James Madison DeWolf."

Fannie sat straight with one hand fisted on her hymnal. The other still clenched the gold cross. Tears flowed down her face. She didn't wipe them away.

"First Sergeant Frederick Hohmeyer, Company E."

Mary Hohmeyer gasped and slid from her chair with a loud thump onto the hardwood floor. Two men helped her out of the room.

"Private William B. Crisfield, Company L."

Mary Crisfield sobbed and moaned loudly, doubled over the hymnal in her lap.

"Trumpeter Thomas Francis McElroy, Company E."

Nora McElroy bolted from her chair with a blood-curdling scream. "No!" Whirling hysterically, still shrieking, she tore at her hair, ripped open the top of her dress and clawed bright red marks across her chest. Marie McLaughlin jumped to her aid, but she jerked away. "Get away, dirty squaw!" She lashed at Marie's face with her nails, missed and tumbled over the back of her chair. Flat on her back, her wild eyes fixed on Little Fish and the two younger braves. "Savages! Bloody savages!" she screamed, scrambling on all fours toward the Indians. Several men pulled her up and hurried her out the front door. Her shrieks and wails grew more frantic as they half-pulled, half-carried her across the parade ground into the laundry building.

Fannie's darting eyes found Marie McLaughlin's distraught face. Her husband sat stoically next to her. The Fergusons and Hunts were clearly concerned for her. In the back of the room, Chief Little Fish's weathered face reflected deep sorrow. Her eyes locked briefly with Arousing Hawk's, and then the young brave hurried out.

◇ ◇ ◇

"You have to leave your quarters tomorrow," General Hunt told Fannie that evening.

"My husband warned me, if anything were to happen . . ." Fannie choked, regained her composure and continued. Barely audible: "Wives are camp followers. We have no rights."

"The Fergusons want you to stay with them for as long as you want."

It was hot in the cot by Jimmie's crib that night, but she still needed the comforting feel of her sheet and cover. "I promised you I would be brave," she whispered. "I don't think I can do it, James. I want to die. I want to be with you."

When Jimmie cried, she burrowed more deeply into the covers. Edna came in and took the boy.

The sun was hot and bright when her friend parted the curtains and pulled the sheet back. "I have biscuits in the warmer. There's butter, honey and tea."

Fannie pulled the sheet back over her head. She didn't want biscuits, didn't want tea. She wanted James. She refused to get up for the noon meal. Her nightgown was soaked with perspiration. She didn't care.

"Fannie, get up. It's time for supper. You must eat."

She stayed curled under the covers.

Edna sighed and left. Fannie wanted to drift off to endless sleep, but she had no sleep left. She whispered: "Dear James, I know what you would want." She pulled her heavy legs over the side of the bed.

◖◗◖◗◖◗

"Wenonah is in mourning for your husband. She's chopped her hair and has dressed in rags," Marie McLaughlin told Fannie the next day.

"I must see her."

"She's not seeing anyone, but Little Fish would like you to visit. There's something else you must know. Little Fish's son, Arousing Hawk, has taken DeWolf as his last name to honor your husband for saving his mother. His wife will have the name, too. All of their children and all following generations will be called DeWolfe, registered with an 'e' added at the end because my husband thinks Wolf is too 'Indian.'"

"I don't know what to say," Fannie said.

They left before sunrise while the air was cool. Fannie wore a winter-weight black mourning dress, black hat and black veil loaned to her by Edna Ferguson. The reservation was a wasteland. The Indians' gardens and fields of potatoes and corn had been scorched by the blazing sun, withered by drought, and denuded by beetles and grasshoppers. They passed a row of bushy trees, where women picked berries and placed them in bags slung over their shoulders.

"Chokecherries," Marie said, "they harvest them when the red fruit turns deep purple, almost black. If hunters are successful this fall, they'll slice and dry the meat, pound it and then make pemmican by mixing heated fat and crushed cherries into the pulverized meat. If the men find little game, the women will dry the bitter fruit and they will eat it through the winter. They fear it might be all they have."

"Surely, now that your husband is here," Fannie started.

"My husband's told them they'll be fed but they don't believe. They're frightened, Missus DeWolf. They're in mourning because of what happened on the Little Bighorn. They mourn for the dead— Indians and soldiers. They mourn for themselves, too. They fear the government will starve and kill them now."

"Yet Chief Little Fish wants to see me?" Fannie asked, her voice quavering with emotion.

"To acknowledge what you and your husband have done. Your husband saved Wenonah, and you stood up to Beckwith."

They sat around a fire near Little Fish's tepee with several dozen Dakota men, women and children. Little Fish, with Arousing Hawk by his side, looked toward the sky and recited a Dakota prayer:

Grandfather, Great Spirit, you have been always,
and before you nothing has been. There is no one
to pray to but you. The star nations all over the
heavens are yours, and yours are the grasses of the earth.
You are older than all need, older than all pain and prayer.

Grandfather, Great Spirit, look upon your children,
The Spirit Lake Dakota, that they may face the winds
and walk the good road to the day of quiet.

Grandfather, Great Spirit, fill us with the light.
Give us the strength to understand and eyes to see.
Teach us to walk the soft earth as relatives to all that live.
Help us, for without you we are nothing.

Arousing Hawk rose and looked directly at Fannie. "We welcomed you and your husband into our tepees for we looked through your eyes and saw your true hearts. You are a good woman, your husband a good man. Like your husband, you are a healer. So now I have taken your husband's name, as you have, to honor both of you as both of you have honored us."

A letter from Montana arrived in August:

Camp on the mouth of the Big Horn River, Montana, Ter.
July 28th 1876

Dear Madam:

You have heard the sad—sad news of the terrible disaster of the Custer fight—and the saddest (to you) of all—the death of your husband Dr. DeWolf. He and myself were very good friends. We tented and messed together were riding side by side during the charge and when the retreat was ordered I was just behind him as we crossed the river. I saw him safe across and then he turned up a ravine a little to my left, which was the last I saw of my friend and companion—alive. As soon as we reached the bluff, I found he was missing and soon found his body, which I buried the next day. I know it will be a great relief to you when I say that his body was not mutilated in the least—that he was not scalped or his clothes even taken.

The Indians had stolen his revolver but not troubled him otherwise. I have collected all of his things that I could find and hold them subject to your order as soon as I arrive in Bismarck, D.T. where I have sent some of them and where I will be as soon as the campaign is over.

Please address me at Bismarck, D.T. where your letters will be forwarded.

I have several letters addressed to him which are evidently from you and which I will forward to you with the other articles.

You have my heartfelt sympathies in your terrible affliction and if there is anything I can do please let me know.

Very Respectfully
Your obt. servt.
H.R. Porter
A.A. Surg. U.S.A

Fannie called on the Hunts that evening. "You've been most gracious, everyone has, but it's time for me to leave."

"I'll always cherish our hours of companionship and good times at the piano," the commanding officer's wife said.

"You've taught me so much with your natural goodness and grace." Fannie started to cry. "I don't know how I would have made it through these past weeks without you and the others. You're all dear friends, but it's become too painful here at Totten without my husband."

"What will you do, where will you go?"

"I'll stay with my sister and her husband in Ohio, at least for a while."

"An Army wagon will take you to Jamestown. Your travel from there will be paid from our officers' family welfare fund," General Hunt said.

The next morning, Fannie paid one last visit to the quarters she'd shared with James. The place had been warm last November. Fires crackled and candles cast a friendly glow. Now, in smothering heat, it was empty and void of human warmth. She clasped her hands over her empty womb. "I need to get out of this place, out of Dakota."

The married officers and their wives, the bachelor officers and the McLaughlins waited in a farewell line. The wagon with her belongings and a covered carriage stood in front of the hospital. Overwhelmed, "A carriage?" was all she could say.

"You can't travel in an open buckboard, not under the hot sun in heavy mourning clothes," General Hunt said.

Fannie offered a gloved hand to each officer and both hands to each woman. She drew strength from her fellow camp followers.

"Keep up with your piano. It will help," the commanding officer's wife said.

"I will miss you, dear friend." Edna squeezed Fannie's hands.

"The Spirit Lake Dakota will never forget you or your husband, nor will I," Marie said.

19

When I lost my baby it felt like God reached into my chest, broke my heart and took my baby, but he forgot to take me too. Instead I am left here with the hurt, pain and absolute living hell of a broken heart and shattered dreams.
—Anonymous

The last stretch of rail line in Ohio was closed for repairs and by the time Fannie boarded the stage to Norwalk, there was only one seat left—with two peddlers in the wildly bouncing rear. The cigar-smoking skinny one with rotten teeth and foul breath sat thigh-to-thigh with her. His obese partner took up the other half of the bench.

Fannie cut short the skinny one's odoriferous attempts at conversation and leaned as far as she could with her nose pointed toward the stage's open side. Watching the sun crest the eastern horizon, she vowed not to let the discomforts and indignities get her down. But her heavy mourning dress held heat like an oven and the road was rough—cut and pocked with ruts and holes and baked rock hard by the sun.

During their noon stop, she ate an apple and a biscuit washed down with water and wiped her face and neck with a damp rag. On the road again, the spine-cracking ride and draining heat dragged her down. She thought about James, gone forever from her life. And she thought about their baby, gone forever, too.

When the stage finally reached Norwalk, she nearly fell exiting the coach. Her sister and brother-in-law, Emma and David Hall, rushed to her aid and helped her into their carriage.

"Fannie, are you all right?" Emma asked. "You're white as a ghost!"

Fannie didn't reply, so Emma spoke for her. "It's the heat, and that awful, heavy dress."

At their home, David and Emma helped her out of the carriage and up to the second-floor spare bedroom, where Emma started unfastening her dress.

"I'll get water," David said, quickly departing.

Fannie curled on top of the covers with her hands clutched over her stomach and sobbed and moaned deliriously. "I lost our baby!"

"You were *expecting*?" Emma asked.

"James never knew."

David returned with a glass and full pitcher and left the room again, closing the door on his way out. Emma held the glass to Fannie's lips and then helped her out of her heavy dress. Fannie fell into a deep sleep, and Emma went downstairs.

"She's been through a horrible ordeal, David, apparently discovering she was with child after her husband left, and then losing the baby before she could tell him. First the baby taken away, and then her husband, I can't imagine."

Fannie slept the rest of the day and through the night. Her sister helped her sit up for more water as mid-morning sun streamed through a bedroom window. Weak and emotionally drained, Fannie's limbs were too heavy to move. She declined food and fell back asleep.

Day after day, her sister's pleas for her to get out of bed went unanswered. The Halls' doctor examined her and told them that Fannie was suffering from melancholia so deep she might simply fade away. "You must get her to eat, and keep trying to get her out of bed."

Fannie allowed Emma to roll her onto her side, clean her and care for her the way she had wanted to care for Mitzdorf, although the soldier wouldn't allow her to perform any intimate cleaning tasks. Ghostly pale, she drifted closer to death, not caring. She would never see James again, not in this life. Only death would bring them back together. She would never hold or care for their baby. She felt relief after the miscarriage. It offered her a chance to start anew with James, without guilt or complications.

Now, she had no reason to live.

Sometimes in dreams, she saw herself in a canoe, drifting in fog on a black-water river, ever closer, to James. She drifted in and out of sleep and dreams until one morning Emma touched her and she looked up into her sister's grief-stricken face and remembered how she had cared and grieved for John Mitzdorf. She remembered her promise to James. If anything were to happen to him, she would be brave. He was gone; there was no baby, but her promise remained.

She lifted her head. "Emma, help me please."

Emma lifted her sister and hugged her frail, thin body. It took time, and every bit of Emma's and Fannie's combined strength, but she made it to the chamber pot and cleaned herself with Emma's help. She renewed her vow to James as she collapsed into bed: No matter what, she would get up every morning and face each day.

At night in the darkness, alone in her bed, she resumed her whispering conversations. "It's so hard, James, hard to go on without you, without our baby. I know, where you are now, you must know about the baby. I want to be with both of you. I have no reason to live, but know I must. God will decide when it's time for me to be with you again."

A week later she told him she had regained enough strength to spend her days in the Halls' parlor with Emma. "I've placed an ad in the paper for work making hats and dresses. I told Emma and David I want to pay what I can toward my room and board. They protested, of course, but I insisted. I know it's what you would do."

Two weeks later: "I have plenty of work to keep me busy. I have a dress form and hat stand. I work in the parlor, and Emma keeps me company. It helps, having her as my dear companion, but James, oh how I miss you."

David and Emma's small, two-story house at 58 East Seminary Street became her refuge. She worked all week, went shopping with Emma on Saturdays and to church with David and Emma on Sundays. Sometimes, on warm sunny days, they strolled downtown for ice cream or a phosphate.

Gradually, Emma drew her out with questions about James and their time together in Oregon, Boston and Dakota. Talking about him helped. "He was such a wonderful man. He loved me so much, sometimes too much," she said, smiling. "His jealousy made me angry at times, not any more."

One brisk September day, she took Emma to her room and opened her trunk. Digging to the bottom, she took out the black yarn and unfinished sweater.

"I haven't wanted to look at this since I packed it at Fort Totten. I was making it for James's birthday next January. I'd like to finish it now and give it to David."

"I know he will be honored, and proud to wear it," Emma smiled.

She received a second latter from Doctor Porter in late September:

Bismarck, D.T.
Sept. 14, 1876
Mrs. Fanny J. DeWolf

Dear Madam
I returned a few days ago & found your letter waiting. Yes he was killed instantly— he was shot in the left breast and four times in the face— probably the first shot in the breast caused instant death as it was in the region of the heart. The other 4 shots I think were fired from his own revolver after he was dead by the Indian who killed him & who stole the revolver.
The Dr. never said anything which indicated that he feared any

harm would befall him yet sometimes I thought he appeared rather sad and once or twice it entered my mind that he had a presentiment of that kind. . . .

In regard to his pay I do not know— am under the impression that he drew pay in advance as quite a number of officers did—perhaps you know all about it.

Please let me hear from you again on receipt of the things. I hope they will reach you safe & if there is anything I can do please let me know.

Very Respectfully Yours
H.R. Porter
If you have a photograph of the Doctor to spare
I should prize it very highly. H.R.P.

● ▪ ○ ▪ ●

Funeral of Surgeon DeWolf
The remains of James M. DeWolf, M.D. assistant surgeon of the regular army, who was slain in the Custer massacre on the Little Big Horn river, Dakota Territory, June 25th, 1876, arrived at this place on the 9 o'clock train from the west, Wednesday morning. Mr. M.L. Chappell took charge of the remains, and after carefully unpacking them at his rooms, conveyed them to the residence of Mr. D.T. Hall, 58 East Seminary Street, brother-in-law of the deceased, where appropriate funeral services were conducted by the Rev. Mr. Mills, of the Baptist church, at 4 o'clock in the afternoon. A number of citizens and sympathizing friends assisted in the last sad rites for one who fell in defense of his country, and now sleeps in our beautiful Woodlawn Cemetery.

—The "Norwalk Reflector," August 8, 1877

Standing erect on the depot platform, Fannie wore her black dress and black hat with a black veil over her face. The jeweled, engraved gold cross was around her neck. The train screeched in steam and a handsome man in a dark gray suit, vest, white shirt and white bow tie stepped down from a passenger car and strode directly to Fannie.

"Missus DeWolf, you are more beautiful than the photo Doctor DeWolf showed me so many times." Doctor Henry Porter bowed and kissed her extended hand.

"It was so kind of you to stop on the way to your wedding in Oberlin," Fannie replied. "What you did for my husband after he was killed, what you have done for me, your letters, and now this, it's overwhelming."

Fannie slipped a white lace hanky under her veil and wiped her eyes, feeling an unexpected wave of resentment behind the grief. Why did James die when this doctor was spared? She pushed the feeling back.

After the service, a horse-drawn hearse led the funeral procession to Woodlawn Cemetery, where David and town dignitaries removed the flag-draped casket and placed it on a stand. Soldiers fired a jarring three-volley salute, removed the flag, ceremoniously folded it and presented it to Fannie.

James's remains were re-interred in a Hall family plot. That night, Fannie folded her mourning dress and placed it in her trunk. She put the hat over the neck and the folded flag over the waist. Finally, she lovingly placed the medical book with the dried, pink rosebud over the fabric that had covered her heart.

She saw Porter off the next morning.

"Here is the photograph of my husband you requested, and a wedding gift for you and Miss Charlotte Viets," she said, handing Porter a wrapped package. "It's something I made while at Fort Totten."

Porter squeezed her hand and brushed it with his lips. "If you need anything at any time, Missus DeWolf," he said.

Boarding the train, he turned on the steps and tipped his gray bowler hat. Fannie said clearly, so he could read her lips: "Thank you, doctor."

20

Waterville

Comfort! Comfort scorned of devils. This is truth the poet sings. That a sorrow's crown of sorrow is remembering happier things
> *—Entry from Fannie's diary, Nov. 21, 1883*

"**T**he Columbian House in Waterville is looking for an upstanding young woman to open a dress and millinery shop," Fannie said, reading a notice in the *Norwalk Reflector*. "I might apply."

"Every lady in Norwalk wants a dress made by Frances Jane DeWolf. If you feel you must be on your own, find another place here," Emma replied.

"I can't explain it, Emma, I cherish my time with you, but leaning on you, I need to get away. Waterville isn't far."

Emma and David took Fannie to Woodlawn Cemetery the evening before her departure and waited at a distance while she laid pink roses on James's grave.

She kissed three fingertips and touched his name carved in the obelisk monument she'd purchased with her Army widow's money. "I love you, dear, and I know you love me. Please, don't worry.

Your brother has agreed to pay me for the land you were buying, so I'll be fine. I think Erastus is pleased to have all the land."

Her shop in the Columbian House at the corner of River Road and Farnsworth was more than she'd hoped for—a spacious room on the second floor with three large windows. Doctor Samuel Downs, the handsome young physician with an office next door, welcomed her and gave her a tour of the three-story building, a solid structure framed with native black walnut, sided with white-painted clapboard and finished inside with walnut woodwork and doors.

"It's the best business place in Waterville," he said while showing her the third-floor ballroom. "The food and service in the first-floor inn are excellent, which draws people here. The Maumee River is a pleasant place for picnics and strolls. We share the second floor with a druggist and a school, which keeps the place lively. There's a jail cell at the other end of our floor, but you needn't worry. It confines drunks and prisoners in transit. There's never any trouble."

Back in his office, he nervously cleared his throat. "Everyone knows of your tragic loss. My wife and I live just across the street. We would be honored if you would join us for dinner."

May Downs met them at the door.

"I hope you didn't go to too much trouble," Fannie said.

"Don't be silly," May replied. "Please accept our condolences for your loss."

As Fannie was leaving, May told her, "I'm having a dinner party Thursday evening at seven o'clock. You must come. My sister, Frances, everybody calls her Frank, is anxious to meet you."

The dinner was a formal affair—roast pork, peas and boiled baby red potatoes lightly buttered with parsley, followed by cherry pie and ice cream. Fannie sat between May's sister, Frances Isham, and the town's most eligible bachelor, Elijah Dodd. He owned a farm at the edge of town, a peach orchard on a Maumee River island near the Columbian house, and a blacksmith and carriage shop downtown. He was charming and handsome and clearly interested in her, but he drank too much wine with the meal and too much brandy with dessert. Fannie was more interested in May's sister, who radiated youthful energy and lifted her spirits.

"Elijah Dodd couldn't take his eyes off you!" Frank said after supper as they strolled around town. "My sister is a compulsive matchmaker. That's why you were seated between him and me. She matched us as bosom friends and you with Elijah Dodd as your potential suitor."

"I'm not interested in marrying again. I wish you could have known James. He would have done anything for me."

"I hope a man loves me that way one day."

They stopped by the river and listened to its flow. It was a dark, moonless night.

"James died near a river in the wilderness. I wanted to die, too, when I learned he'd been killed. I don't care much now, one way or the other," Fannie said softly.

"Beastly savages!"

"Not all of them," Fannie whispered. "Not the Indians near the fort where he was stationed. They were in such sad condition. James treated many. I went with him to their camps as his nurse."

"You went to the wild Indian camps?" Frank asked, wide-eyed.

"They weren't so wild," Fannie said. "There was a Sioux chief, Little Fish, whose wife was deathly ill. She recovered after James treated her. Her son took DeWolf as his last name to honor my husband."

"But the ones who killed your husband," Frank began.

"Did unspeakable things to many of the men," Fannie finished for Frank, "although my husband didn't suffer any such abominations. Their acts were inexcusable, but I know from having been in Dakota that our government has wronged the Indians, even the peaceful ones. There was a boy, a grandson of Little Fish, the last time I held him in my arms he was starved, listless and light as a bird." Fannie wiped her eyes.

"You've been through so much. I've lived all my nineteen years here in Waterville. I can't *imagine* making friends with savages, can't imagine holding a starving heathen baby, can't imagine how you must have felt when you learned your husband had been killed."

"I was nineteen, your age, when we married. My years with him, I can't explain. Nothing will ever be the same."

•◦•◦•

Life spread before me a cold calm sea, over which my bark was to glide, on a chill, drear voyage, that had now, no aim, or purpose.
—Entry from Fannie's personal diary, January, 1878

Frank wasn't quite the friend Fannie had hoped for. Her exuberant peaks were followed by dark depression. When Frank bubbled with energy, Fannie felt she could live through anything with courage if not joy. When her friend plunged, Fannie fell with her.

On a cold, gloomy morning during one low period, she felt she couldn't keep her promise to James. She'd stay in bed just like Frank. She wouldn't eat or drink, and would drift away to the next world where she would be with James.

Late that morning, she heard a knock at her bedroom door. She didn't care. May called her name several times and finally came in. "You must get up," she commanded with the firmness of a school matron. "My sister has a malady of the spirit. She's suffered bouts of melancholia for years. You are wallowing in self pity."

"What do you know? Who have you lost?" Fannie asked.

"You're strong, Fannie. You know you are."

May left and Fannie thought about how James must feel, watching her now. With considerable effort, she got up and went to her shop. After closing, she went to the Downs' home, where Frank was secluded in the spare bedroom with the shades pulled.

"She's not seeing anyone, not even me," May said.

Fannie went in, anyway. "Sometimes I feel I can't go on," she told Frank. "This morning was one of those times. Your sister helped me, now I must help you."

Frank didn't respond. Weeks passed, and then one day out of

the blue she breezed into Fannie's shop, radiant as ever. Two weeks later she was bedridden again. Fannie couldn't take it. She bought a stage ticket and went to see Emma, who'd been begging her to visit and make her a dress.

Frank wrote:

My Darling! How I wish I was "Nearer to thee" . . . but I will wait . . . and try to be patient and content until I see the loving friend whose dear sweet sisterly counsel and sympathy I miss so much. . . . I hope to mercy you've finished that dress of yours which you prize so much higher than you do your friends in Waterville—save one or two. . . . How often I wonder what my sweet soul sister is doing or thinking of just now.

● ◦ ● ◦ ●

Frank was bubbling with energy when Fannie returned. She spent much of her time in the dress shop, dramatically declaring their hopes and their dreams, their troubles and their poor prospects for a bright future.

Elijah Dodd called frequently, too. His intense, year-long courtship culminated one night in late March, 1879, when he took Fannie to the Columbian House Inn for supper and asked her to marry him. They were wed on June 10. Frank was maid of honor.

On February 21, 1881, Fannie gave birth to a boy. They named him Verne Adams Dodd. He had Elijah's brown hair and brown eyes. Fannie marveled at how beautiful he was, but there was a touch of sadness, too. She and James never had their baby, never had a chance to stay another year in Dakota to continue their work with the Devils Lake Sioux.

Samuel and May Downs held a celebratory reception when Fannie was sufficiently recovered from childbirth.

"He's so beautiful, Faun," Frank told her. "Verne Adams Dodd, the name of a president, or maybe a chief justice!" she gushed "Don't you think?"

"He won't be a politician or judge. He'll be a doctor just like . . ." Fannie caught herself. No one seemed to notice her slip except for Frank.

"Doctor Verne Adams Dodd," Frank blurted out loudly enough for everyone to hear.

"Doctor like hell!" Elijah glared at Frank and Fannie. "He'll be a businessman just like his father! Businessmen make the wheels of industry and commerce turn. Doctors are glorified lackeys who provide a simple service like shoe shine boys!"

"Elijah!" Fannie responded.

"By the time he's thirty, our son will own all of Waterville and half the county!"

"Elijah! You . . ."

"Oh hush up, Fannie! You're such a stick in the mud! Have a drink and loosen up!"

She put her arm through his and whispered, "You've had enough to drink."

He jerked away and emptied his glass.

Fannie took baby Verne to her shop, and when she wasn't busy, she held him in her arms and read to him. She talked to James, too:

"Verne is a wonderful boy," she told him one day. "He soaks up everything, remembers everything and has such a good nature. He tests me, as all children do, but never in a malicious way. He thinks he should be able to do everything grownups do. I've caught him several times trying to walk instead of crawl down the stairs. He's taken some tumbles. He cries, but just a little, and he gets right up." Fannie sighed. "I hoped Elijah would love him the way I know you would have loved *our* child, but he ignores Verne most of the time and only talks about what he will do for his businesses."

Frances Isham married Alfred Chantler in Waterville on July 24, 1883, and left for St. Paul, where he was manager of the United Press Association bureau. Fannie was happy for her friend, but she felt a sense of foreboding, too, and wrote in her diary:

She was happy now: and happiness did not come often enough to be voluntarily flung aside. The old, old half sophisticated, half reckless arguments with which we silence the voices in our souls when they warn us to escape from peril; and then, when too late, marvel that we could have been so deaf to their persistency.

Frank wrote Fannie on February 3, 1884 that she was with child and making the most of the short time she had left before being "closeted up" in her last months of pregnancy. She had been out sleighing with Al. She had been to the ice rink but did not skate. She was making clothes for herself and her expected baby.

Frank gave birth to a girl on April 14 and named her after her sister—May Lillian Chantler.

"You and Elijah must join us for supper to celebrate," May told Fannie after receiving the news.

Elijah had three glasses of wine with the meal and was about to refill his brandy glass afterwards when Fannie said, "It's time to go, Elijah. It's past Verne's bedtime." She slid the glass out of his reach.

"Go on home," he said outside. "I've some things to take care of at the shop."

"I know what you're doing."

"What's that, Fannie, what am I doing?" he replied with sarcasm.

Three-year-old Verne looked up at his mom and then at his dad.

"I know what you keep in your desk. The drinking has to stop, Elijah."

"I told you I've got work. Now go home!"

After midnight, Fannie heard him stagger through the front door and up the stairs. He climbed into bed, threw a heavy arm over her and tried to pull her nightgown up. She pushed him away. He tried again, and Fannie went to Verne's room.

◇ ◇ ◇ ◇

A telegram from St. Paul arrived on April 23, 1884
"Dear Fannie,
Frank passed on to a better place late yesterday. Childbirth too much. Just faded away. With God now.
                                                                   Al Chantler"

Fannie felt a dark veil begin to fall. She dropped into a chair in her shop and breathed deeply. She couldn't, wouldn't let Frank pull her down again, she swore, not even in death.

Things grew worse between her and Elijah. If it weren't for her son, she might have despaired.

"I've stayed with you for the sake of Verne. I'm warning you," she said one morning while placing a plate of eggs, biscuits and bacon in front of him, "if you continue your drinking and abusive language, I will leave you, and take Verne with me."

Elijah pushed the plate violently across the table, knocking his full coffee cup and scattering eggs and biscuits. The plate shattered on the hardwood floor.

"You!" he shouted. "You're a woman of standing because of me!" He started toward Fannie with his fists clenched, then stopped himself.

"You hold your voice down! Your son is upstairs!"

"You think you're *so* much better, too good for me after your precious Indian-fighter doctor!" Elijah shouted and moved threateningly toward Fannie.

"How dare you!" She slapped him hard. "Get out of here! Go to your shop!"

"You're the curse of me! You are the reason I drink!"

"You know that's not true! Everyone in town called you 'Quart a Day Dodd' long before I got here! That's got nothing to do with me or our marriage!"

"You married me for my money. You think I don't know about your precious calendars with the X's, your letters from him, his diaries and your diary, the pressed rose, all hidden under your underwear? Your little shrine, dedicated to your precious doctor, the man who you think died a hero! You're pathetic. I should burn his letters, burn everything!"

"How dare you!"

"Don't try that righteous outrage on me, Fannie! You've got all the comforts of wealth and status you were seeking!"

"I didn't marry you for your money!" Tears welled in Fannie's eyes. "I wanted to love you, Elijah." Her crimson face flushed deeper red. "You don't care how I feel, or how your drinking hurts your son." Fannie struggled for control, and then continued, "If you had loved me, Elijah, if you had loved me as James did, you would have stopped your heavy drinking."

Elijah almost knocked Verne over as he stormed out of the house. Fannie picked him up and hugged him. "I'm sorry. I thought you were upstairs," was all she said.

"What's the matter, Mommy?" was all he said, and she replied, "Don't worry."

Elijah staggered back home after 2 a.m. and passed out next to Fannie. She took her pillow to the parlor floor.

<hr>

"Verne, wake up. We're leaving."

Wise beyond his eleven years, Verne got out of bed and quickly found the clothes he would wear, folded on the chest at the foot of his bed.

"Our suitcases are packed and in the carriage," Fannie said.

Verne slept for a while, leaning against his mother as they rode in pitch darkness. When he woke up, he asked, "Mom, there's something I've been wondering. What was Dad talking about when I was little, you know, that day when he yelled at you during breakfast about your precious Indian-fighting doctor, your letters from him, his diaries and the pressed rose?"

Fannie smiled in the darkness. "Do you ever forget anything?"

"I don't know, I guess some things."

"You know I was married before, and my first husband was killed before I married your father."

"Everybody knows that, Mom. Kids at school are always asking about your famous husband who was killed in the battle at the Little Bighorn. They say things like, 'I wish I was you and my Mom was married to somebody who fought and died with Custer.'"

"It's not something to wish for."

"I know."

"Dying in battle, famous or not, is not something to aspire to."

"I know."

"My first husband loved me above all else, Verne, even more than his own life. So yes, I do have all of the letters he wrote to me during his expedition with the Seventh Cavalry. I have his diaries, too, and the rose blossom he cut for me near Rosebud Creek and pressed in a medical book before he was killed near the Little Bighorn. Would you like me to read from his diary and letters sometime? The writing is hard to decipher sometimes, but I know them practically by heart. I've never shown them to anyone."

"I'd like that very much. Could you tell me stories about him, too?"

"Of course, I would love to."

The black turned to pre-dawn haze, and then the sun rose orange-pink through grand oaks as they approached the estate near Toledo where Fannie had arranged to work as a housekeeper and nanny in return for room, board and a small salary. Mist rose from the estate's warm earth into the crisp fall air.

Her work at the estate was arduous, but her employers were kind to both her and Verne, so she didn't mind. Her son was her pride and joy—an excellent student and a comforting companion who loved listening to her letters from James, his diaries, and stories about their adventures together in Oregon, Boston and Dakota.

Still, the emptiness was never far away. In 1892, the year she worked near Toledo, she wrote in her diary:

> *Life is full of sorrow many a secret grief,*
> *Weighs the heart, to which alas!*
> *Time brings no relief;*
> *Struggles that no friend can share,*
> *Weakness unrevealed*
> *Passion burning fiercer far*
> *Because so close concealed.*
>
> *—F.J.D.*

After a year away, Fannie and Elijah came to an understanding. She and Verne would move back to Waterville, but only so the boy could see his father. She rented two upstairs bedrooms in a small house and reopened her shop at the Columbian House. Elijah paid half the rent and provided additional support for her and Verne, who thrived in high school academics and drama.

"You were wonderful, Verne!" Fannie beamed after his high school's production of *Romeo and Juliet*. "Such a presence on stage, a seasoned actor twice your age couldn't have done better. I'm so proud of you. I know your father is, too."

"He could have stayed and told me himself," Verne said.

"I saw him watching you. He is proud of you."

"I think I'd like to be a professional actor, maybe go to London and study."

"You can do whatever you decide. You know I will support you. All I ask is that you go to medical school first. After that, if you still want to pursue a career on the stage, that's fine with me."

● ● ● ●

"Now, you can pursue your acting career!" Fannie said after Verne's 1903 graduation from medical school in Columbus.

Verne laughed, "You only say that because you know I've been accepted for advanced study at Harvard Medical School."

"In surgery, the specialty Doctor DeWolf grew to love while attending Harvard," Fannie said. "You are quite handsome, you know, in your cap and gown. I imagine you could make the young ladies swoon if you did return to the stage."

"What makes you think I need to be on stage to make the girls swoon?" Verne asked, smiling.

After Harvard, Verne returned to Columbus to teach and establish his surgical practice. He was the one who swooned when he met Nelle May Jacobs. They were married in 1906, and after the ceremony Verne pleaded with Fannie to join them in Columbus.

"You and Father have been separated for so long. You have no family in Waterville, really, no reason to remain there."

"I have Samuel and May and my other friends."

"You know I've missed you," Verne said.

"I've missed you, too. I just never thought about moving."

"I have friends at a fraternity in Columbus, Alpha Sigma Phi. They need a housemother. They've heard me talk about you so much, they think you're the only one for them," Verne said. "They say no one else will do, only Missus Dodd."

Fannie blushed. "I don't think I'm up to being housekeeper and cook for a house full of boisterous young men."

"They have a cook. They clean the house themselves. All you would have to do is provide a motherly influence, a guiding hand," Verne said.

"How badly do they need that?"

"I'll take you there for dinner. You can judge for yourself."

Fannie eventually moved to Columbus, where she offered "a guiding hand" to the fraternity men and watched her son's career and family grow. Her grandson, Verne Adams Jr., was born on January 1, 1908, and her granddaughter, Jane Eleanor, on May 22, 1911.

Both children brought her unexpected joy.

In March 1912, Verne accepted an officer's commission in the U.S. Army Medical Reserve Corps, and for the first time Fannie wasn't sure she approved of her son following James's career path. Would he face death in a war one day?

* * *

Verne stepped into the waiting room still in his surgical clothes, looking tired and worried. "I couldn't come sooner. I was in the middle of surgery. A nurse told me you were here with important news. What's the matter?"

"Nothing's wrong, Verne, but I do have something important to tell you." Her son sat, and she continued. "I've seen a lawyer. I've filed for divorce from your father and he has agreed not to contest."

"So soon?" Verne asked with a smile.

"It's not a joking matter, Verne."

"I know."

The decree was filed in November, 1912, and for the first time in over thirty-six years, Fannie felt free—free of her pain, of her guilt, of her grief and despair. She was one with James again. She realized that Elijah had been right all along. She'd never loved anyone the way she loved James, couldn't love anyone that way—not Verne, whom she loved with all her heart and soul, not Nelle or even her grandchildren.

***

"I'm being called to active duty," Verne, now an Assistant Professor of Surgery at Ohio State University, told Fannie in 1917.

"You won't have to go to Europe, will you?" Fannie asked.

"Not likely," Verne replied. "I'm resigning from the Army and accepting a promotion to Lieutenant Commander in the U.S. Navy Medical Corps. The military wants me to help establish a Navy hospital at Hampton Roads, Virginia."

"Are you sure you won't have to go to Europe?"

"No, Mother, I won't have to go. There are too many young men coming home in need of surgery and medical care. Not that I would have minded duty on the front lines so much, but I know you couldn't stand it."

"I've seen enough war, enough of men maimed and killed, the War Between the States, the Indian wars that took my James, and now this so-called 'Great War,' so many young boys on both sides slaughtered and maimed." Fannie sighed. "How soon do you have to leave?"

"In a month, you must come with us, Mother. You have nothing keeping you here any longer, now that you're no longer working at the fraternity house."

"The boys invite me to Sunday dinner. I'm still a mother to them. I won't be alone."

"They so adore you, I know," Verne said, "but I can't leave you behind, not with the way you've been feeling. I would worry constantly."

"I'll consider it, but only after you've talked with Nelle."

"She says you must come."

●○●○●○●

"The news isn't good, is it," Fannie said.

"It may not be bad. You have a tumor," Verne replied. "I have arranged for you to see a specialist, one of the best, at Harvard. Nelle wants to go with you."

"Back to Boston and Harvard," Fannie said to herself. Her eyes misted.

When they weren't eating or sleeping during their voyage from Virginia to Boston, Fannie and Nelle spent their time on deck in the fresh air. The weather was lovely, clear blue skies and a warm sun during the day followed by a rising moon reflected on the water, and then dazzling bright stars in the black sky.

"The stars out here remind me of Dakota Territory and my night walks with James," Fannie said. "Oh, we had such adventures."

"Verne has told me stories, but I still can't imagine."

"It's hard for me to imagine now."

Fannie felt good and was full of energy during their stay in Boston. She and Nelle went to plays and concerts between examinations and treatments. They sailed back to Virginia with bad news. Her tumor, a blossoming growth shaped like a cauliflower, was inoperable and malignant. She became bedridden not long after their return.

One night, she asked Verne and Nelle to come into her room.

"I want both of you to know, I have been so blessed, from the day I met James when I was a teenager in the Oregon wilderness to this very day with you and my grandchildren, my life has been filled with blessings. I am at peace."

"Mother," Verne said.

"I'm not finished."

Nelle gripped Fannie's hand.

"I never loved anyone but James. I think your father sensed that, Verne. No, that's not fair. I know he sensed it early in our marriage and came to know it with a certainty that must have been very painful for him. It may be why he ignored my pleas about his drinking. Anyway, the day our divorce was final, I felt free. It was as if I had joined James in heaven."

"You don't need to explain," Verne said.

"I'm not finished. When I die, I want to be with James. I want to be buried by his side."

"Of course, Mother."

Fannie died May 19, 1918 at age 65. She was buried next to James at Woodlawn Cemetery in Norwalk, Ohio.

BECKWITH, Paul, Indian agent at the Devils Lake Agency near Fort Totten from September 1875 until July 1, 1876. After his resignation, he moved to Colorado, where he worked as an assayer and mining engineer. In 1886, he moved to Washington, DC, where he became assistant archivist at the Smithsonian Institution and eventually assistant curator in the Anthropology Department. He was 59 when he died in 1907.

BENTEEN, Captain Frederick, Company H commander and battalion commander on scout the day of the battle. James met Benteen at Fort Abraham Lincoln in April and wrote Fannie that he enjoyed his "regular fun" and "easy spoken" manner. He was wounded at the Little Bighorn, retired in 1888 and was 63 when he died in 1898.

BRENNER, Ernst, Fort Totten trader while the DeWolfs were there. Brenner later was placed in charge of the Ojibwa and Metis people's Turtle Mountain Reservation in Dakota. In the early 1890s, he worked with others to strip the Ojibwa and Metis of most of their land. The settlement included a payment of $1 million for the tribe's ten million-acre claim to North Dakota lands, referred to bitterly by the Ojibwa and Metis as the Ten-Cent Treaty.

CALHOUN, First Lieutenant James, Company L commander. He was married to Custer's sister, Margaret. He and James met in the late 1860s at Camp Warner, Oregon, and were reunited when Calhoun arrived at Fort Seward on March 23, 1876. James told Fannie he liked Calhoun "and you would for he is a gentleman." With Custer's column, he was 30 when he was killed at the Little Bighorn.

CLEAR, Private Elihu, Company K. He killed Black Kettle's daughter during the Seventh Cavalry's attack on the Cheyenne chief's camp near the Washita River in 1868. James stopped to help Clear, who was mortally wounded during Reno's retreat. Clear was 32 or 33 when he was killed while climbing a bluff east of the Little Bighorn River.

CUSTER, Lieutenant Colonel George Armstrong, Seventh Cavalry commanding officer. James first saw him at Fort Abraham Lincoln after Custer's testimony in Washington regarding corruption in the War Department. Custer was 36 when he was killed.

DeWOLF, Frances Jane (Downing), born June 16, 1852, married James on Oct. 31, 1871, at Camp Warner, Oregon Territory. She married Elijah Dodd of Waterville, Ohio on June 10, 1879. They had one child, Verne Adams Dodd, born Feb. 21, 1881. She filed for divorce in 1912; the decree was final in November. She was 65 when she died on May 19, 1918. She is buried next to James at Woodlawn Cemetery in Norwalk, Ohio.

DeWOLF, Doctor James Madison, born Jan. 14, 1843, Acting Assistant Surgeon on Reno's staff. He was killed in bluffs east of the Little Bighorn River during Reno's retreat on June 25, 1876. He was 33 when he died.

DODD, Doctor Verne Adams, surgeon and professor. The son of Fannie and Elijah Dodd, he was born Feb. 21, 1881, in Waterville, Ohio. He graduated from Ohio Medical University in 1903, attended advanced classes at Harvard Medical School, and eventually became a surgery professor at Ohio State University, where he was Chairman of the Surgery Department in 1921 and Chief of Staff of the University Hospital from 1922 to 1947. Dodd married Nelle Jacobs in 1906. They had two children, Verne A. Dodd, Jr. and Jane E.

Dodd. Verne Dodd was 76 when he died on Feb. 22, 1957. Dodd Hall, which houses Ohio State's nationally acclaimed University Hospitals Rehabilitation Services, is named for him.

FERGUSON, Doctor James B., Fort Totten post surgeon. James and Fannie met Ferguson and his wife, Edna, when they arrived at Fort Totten in November 1875. The Fergusons had one son, James C. Ferguson, born Oct. 19, 1875, at Fort Totten. On May 19, 1873, Doctor Ferguson signed an amendment of the 1867 treaty between the U.S. government and Wahpeton, Sisseton and Cuthead Sioux, which terminated their land and hunting rights in Dakota Territory outside designated reservations. Ferguson retired from the Army in 1911 and moved with his wife to St. Paul. He was 85 when he died Sept. 2, 1926.

HARBACH, Captain Abram, at Fort Totten with the 20th Infantry while James was there. A career officer and wounded war veteran, he served in Dakota, Texas, Indian Territory and Montana. In 1898, he led two hundred fourteen men to reinforce a detachment engaged in fighting against Ojibwa Indians at Leech Lake, Minn. He also fought in Cuba and in the Philippine-American War. Married to Lilian Otis, he retired in 1902 after over forty years in the U.S. Army. He died at age 92 on Nov. 22, 1933, in Santa Barbara, Calif.

HUNT, Lieutenant Colonel Lewis Cass, Fort Totten commanding officer while the DeWolfs were there. In 1873, Hunt signed an amendment to the 1867 treaty between the U.S. government and Dakota Sioux, which terminated their land and hunting rights outside designated reservations. In 1877, he led an infantry battalion from Fort Totten to Texas, where his battalion pursued cattle thieves on both sides of the Rio Grande and occupied Indian country between the Rio Grande and Pecos rivers. He was promoted to colonel in 1881. Five years later, his wife, Abby, died of cancer at their home in Michigan. He died about six months after her death, in September 1886 at Fort Union, New Mexico, after years of declining health from chronic dysentery. He was 62.

HODGSON, Second Lieutenant Benjamin, Reno's adjutant. Hodgson and Doctor Henry Porter were James's closest friends during the expedition. He was 28 when he was killed on the east bank of the Little Bighorn River during Reno's retreat from the valley.

LITTLE FISH, Dakota Chief, also called Tiowaste, or Good Lodge. Following the 1862 Sioux uprising in Minnesota, Chief Little Fish joined other Indians who fled west to the Dakota prairie to avoid reprisals at the hands of angry white settlers. He led several hundred of his Sisseton Sioux band into Fort Totten, Dakota Territory, in 1867 after nearly five years of starvation, disease and Army harassment. Little Fish was a strong opponent of white settlement of reservation land and remained a chief on the Devils Lake Reservation near Fort Totten until his death in 1919. His son who honored Doctor DeWolf by taking DeWolfe as his last name also lived out his life on what is now called the Spirit Lake Indian Reservation, passing his DeWolfe name on to future generations.

McDOUGALL, Captain Thomas, Company B commander. James and Fannie became close friends with McDougall and his wife, Alice, during their time at Fort Totten. His company escorted the pack train the day of the Little Bighorn battle. He was 64 when he died in 1909.

McLAUGHLIN, James. An assistant to the Devils Lake Indian agent when the DeWolfs arrived at Fort Totten, he was appointed agent in 1876 and became the Standing Rock agent in 1881. In 1890, while at Standing Rock, he ordered the arrest of Sitting Bull, which led to the killing of the Sioux leader during a gun battle with Indian police. McLaughlin left Standing Rock in 1895 when he was appointed inspector for the Bureau of Indian Affairs. During his tenure as inspector, he negotiated numerous agreements that ceded Indian lands to the government or opened them up to white settlement. He stated during negotiations at the Cheyenne River Indian Reservation in South Dakota that it would be "manifestly better for the Indians to have their surplus lands opened to settlement" so that they may "readily acquire white man's civilization and industrious habits." He was 81 and still with the Indian Bureau when he died in 1923.

McLAUGHLIN, Marie, interpreter and author. She married James McLaughlin in Mendota, Minnesota, on Jan. 28, 1864 and moved with him to Devils Lake near Fort Totten in July 1871. Born Dec. 8, 1842 in Wabasha, Minnesota, her father was French Canadian and her mother half Sioux and half Scotch. Her book, *Myths and Legends of the Sioux*, was published in 1916 by the Bismarck Tribune Company. She was 81 when she died in 1924.

PORTER, Doctor Henry, surgeon on Reno's staff. Porter and Second Lieutenant Hodgson were James's closest friends on the expedition. He survived Reno's valley and hilltop fights, exhibiting courage while treating soldiers under heavy fire. He cared for over sixty wounded men, helped with burials and took locks of hair from fallen officers to send to their widows. He wrote several letters to Fannie and collected and sent James's belongings to her. He married Charlotte Viets in September 1877 in Oberlin, Ohio. He was 55 and on a world tour when he died of a heart attack in 1903 near the Taj Mahal. He was buried in Agra, India. A memorial was erected next to his wife's grave in Oberlin.

RENO, Major Marcus, battalion commander. Reno had been in command at Fort Totten three separate times, but James met Reno after his arrival at Fort Abraham Lincoln in April. At the end of the expedition's first day, he wrote Fannie, *Reno, who commands my wing, I cannot like.* Dogged by accusations of cowardice after the Little Bighorn battle, Reno requested an inquiry into his conduct. A military court cleared him in 1879, but the accusations continued, as did Reno's heavy drinking. He was court-martialed in 1879, found guilty of misconduct and dishonorably discharged. He was 54 when he died of cancer in 1889. In 1967, a military review board changed his discharge to honorable and ordered the re-interment of his remains at the Little Bighorn Cemetery.

* *Men With Custer: Biographies of the 7th Cavalry*, edited by Ronald H. Nichols and copyrighted by the Custer Battlefield Historical & Museum Assn., Inc. in 2000, is the primary source for biographies of members of the Seventh Cavalry.

Doctor Verne Adams Dodd was 60 in 1941 when he began transcribing his mother's letters from James, written during his 1876 journey to the Little Bighorn River with Custer and the rest of the Seventh Cavalry. He transcribed Doctor DeWolf's expedition diary as well. The experience must have brought back fond boyhood memories of his mother's tales about her trip to Oregon as a teen-ager, where she met and married Doctor DeWolf, their times together in Boston, where he went to Harvard Medical School, and at Fort Totten in Dakota, where they lived together and where she stayed when he left for the campaign against the "hostile Sioux."

Later in 1941, Dodd initiated correspondence with Edward S. Luce, superintendent of Custer Battlefield National Cemetery. He made several visits to the battlefield in following years, and eventually donated the diary and all of the letters to the National Park Service. They are part of the historical collection at what is now called the Little Bighorn Battlefield National Monument.

In an early donation cover letter to Luce, dated September 23, 1941, he wrote: *There is enclosed a faded picture of old Fort Totten on Devil's Lake, where my mother remained during the Custer scouting expedition. You will note that I have mounted the letter from Col. Mike Sheridan, which tells mother of the exhumation of* her husband's body, together with the lock of his hair, in which some of the clay still clings and a button from his vest. The small booklets containing part of his diary I had copied in typewritten form, thinking it might be helpful to you, as his writing is somewhat difficult to decipher.

In addition to these enclosures there are a few letters of many that he wrote mother. These were selected because they contained interesting sidelights on the activities of the expedition. I have retained other letters that make occasional reference to occurrences of this scout which may be of some interest to you and which after reading again I may decide to send on.

Sincerely yours,
V.A. Dodd, M.D.

Luce replied in a letter dated October 28, 1941 that the letters *will be valuable relics in the Museum when it is constructed and in the meantime I am taking measures to preserve them. They are being microfilmed and will be kept in a fire-proof safe.*

He added:

The letters are most certainly valuable to get the sidelights of events leading up to the battle, especially the letter the good doctor wrote about the "whiskey-traders" arriving. This clinches or corroborates certain testimony in the Reno Inquiry, 1879, relative to drunkenness. There were several remarks made as to certain officers that had liquor in their possession at the time of the battle and it was hard to see how they could travel from Fort Lincoln towards the battlefield and still have a few bottles left. . . .

Just as soon as I am able to make copies of those articles which you desired to have returned I shall be happy to do so, and I trust also, that I may have the pleasure of seeing you here next summer.

Dodd later wrote to Luce:

I doubt whether any man in the group wrote more frequently and intimately back home than did Dr. DeWolf, in addition to keeping a diary. You have doubtless noted that he wrote every day once, and sometimes two or three times. Husbands of five years standing seldom do that today!

Bibliography

Published Sources

Ambrose, Stephen E. *Crazy Horse and Custer*. New York, 1975.

Berger, Thomas. *Little Big Man*. New York, 1964.

Brennan, M.H. *North Dakota. The Catholic Encyclopedia, Vol. XI*. New York, 1911.

Brown, Dee. *Bury My Heart at Wounded Knee*. New York, 1970.

Bruner Eales, Anne. *Army Wives on the American Frontier, Living by the Bugles*. Boulder, CO., 1996.

Camp, Gregory S. *The Dispossessed: The Ojibwa and Metis of Northwest North Dakota*, article in *North Dakota History, Journal of the Northern Plains*. Bismarck, 2003.

Campbell, Midge. *The Letters of Frances Lillian "Frank" (Isham) Chantler (1858-1884) and Frances Jane "Fannie" (Downing) DeWolf Dodd (1852-1918), Written Between 11 Oct. 1878 & 23 Mar. 1884*. Waterville, Ohio, 1981.

Carroll, John M., editor. *The Benteen-Goldin Letters on Custer and His Last Battle*. New York, 1974.

Childress, Joel Patrick. *Doctor Samuel Overton, Pioneer Doctor of Old Canton, Texas: Vintage Medical Ledgers Perused*, article published at www.rootsweb.com. Tyler, Texas, 2000.

Connell, Evan S. *Son of the Morning Star*. New York, 1984.

Convis, Charles. *The Honor of Arms: A Biography of Myles W. Keogh*. Tucson, 1990.

Custer, Elizabeth B. *Boots and Saddles*. Norman, Okla., 1961.

DeWolfe, Jerome William. *Wakpa Minisota!*. Lincoln, NE, 2005.

Eastman, Doctor Charles A. *The Story of the Little Big Horn*, article in *The Chautauquan*, Plainfield, N.J., July, 1900.

Eastman, Doctor Charles A. *The Woman Winona, the Woman-Child,* published in *Old Indian Days.* Seattle, 1997.

Federici, Richard. *Sgt. Daniel Kanipe.* Mohican Press/Richard Federici. 1998.

Ft. Totten Review, newspaper published by pupils of the Fort Totten Indian School. Article entitled, *Address by Pres. Worst of the N.D. Agricultural College.* May,1911 issue.

Ft. Totten Review. Article entitled, *At Old Fort Totten, A Brief Narrative of Early Days at the Fort.* June, 1913 issue.

Friends of Fort Totten Historic Site. *The Spirit Lake Dakota People.* Fort Totten, N.D.,2000.

Graham, Colonel W.A. *The Custer Myth, A Source Book of Custeriana.* New York, 1953.

Gray, Doctor John S. *Medical Service on the Little Big Horn Campaign,* article in *The Westerners Brand Book.* Chicago, January 1968.

Gray, Doctor John S. *Veterinary Service on Custer's Last Campaign,* article in *Kansas Historical Quarterlies,* Kansas State Historical Society. Topeka, 1977.

Hammer, Kenneth, editor. *Custer in '76, Walter Camp's Notes on the Custer Fight.* Provo, Utah, 1976.

Heski, Thomas M. *The Trail to Heart River,* article in *Research Review, the Journal of the Little Big Horn Associates.* El Paso, 1995.

Jeffords, Christine. *Doctors, Healers, and Health: The State of Medicine in the Old West,* article at freepages.genealogy.rootsweb.com.

Kelly, Carla. *The Buffalo Carcass on the Company Sink: Sanitation at a Frontier Army Fort,* article in *North Dakota History, Journal of the Northern Plains.* Bismarck, 2003.

Kneeland, Jonathan. *On Some Causes Tending to Promote the Extinction of the Aborigines of America,* in *Transactions of the American Medical Association, Vol. 15,* 1964.

Luce, Edward S., editor. *The Diary and Letters of Dr. James M. DeWolf, Acting Assistant Surgeon, U.S. Army; His Record of the Sioux Expedition of 1876 as Kept Until His Death.* Bismarck, 1958.

McLaughlin, James. *My Friend the Indian,* Cambridge, 1926.

McLaughlin, James. *An Account of Sitting Bull's Death. Archives of the West,* Philadelphia, 1891.

McLaughlin, Marie L. *Myths and Legends of the Sioux*. Bismarck, N.D., 1916.

Michno, Gregory F. *Lakota Noon: The Indian Narrative of Custer's Defeat*. Missoula, MT, 1997.

Miller, David Humphreys. *Custer's Fall*. New York, 1957.

Moore, Rex, editor. *Dakota Cowboy Soldier, a collection of documented letters written by Michael Vetter, U.S. Army—7th Cavalry Regiment*. Fort Totten, N.D. no copyright date.

Murray, Earl. *Ghosts of the Old West*. Chicago, 1988.

Nichols, Ronald H, editor. *Men With Custer: Biographies of the 7th Cavalry*. Hardin, Mont., 2000.

Norwalk Reflector. Newspaper article dated Aug. 8, 1877, entitled *Funeral of Surgeon DeWolf*. 1877.

Peterson, Doctor Edward S. *Surgeons of the Little Big Horn*, article in *The Westerners Brand Book*. Chicago, 1974.

Pfaller, the Reverend. Louis. *The Forging of an Indian Agent*, article in *North Dakota History, Journal of the Northern Plains*. Bismarck, 1967.

Porter, Henry R., brief biography and his account of Little Bighorn battle. *Compendium of History and Biography of North Dakota*. Chicago, 1900.

Remele, Larry, editor. *Fort Totten Military Post and Indian School 1867-1959*. Bismarck, 1986.

Reno, Marcus A. *Report on the Battle of Little Big Horn. Annual Report of the Secretary of War*. Washington, D.C. 1876.

Schlissel, Lillian. *Women's Diaries of the Westward Journey*. New York, 1982.

Scott, Douglas D.; Willey, P.; Connor, Melissa A. *They Died with Custer*. Norman, Okla., 1998.

Sklenar, Larry. *To Hell with Honor, Custer and the Little Bighorn*. Norman, Okla., 2000.

Southwest Parks & Monuments Association. *Reno-Benteen Entrenchment Trail*. Crow Agency, Mont., 1999.

Streeter Aldrich, Bess. *The Lieutenant's Lady*. New York, 1942.

Viola, Herman J. *Little Bighorn Remembered, The Untold Indian Story of Custer's Last Stand*. New York, 1999.

Wilbur, C. Keith, M.D. *Civil War Medicine 1861-1865*. Guilford, Ct., 1995.

Other Sources

Bureau of Catholic Indian Missions Records. *Bureau and Commission Correspondence, Dakota Territory, Fort Totten, Devil's Lake Reservation, 1875-1880.* Letters on microfilm, Special Collections and Archives, Marquette University Libraries.

DeWolf, Frances Jane "Fannie"; *Autograph Book and Diary,* undated, late 1870s to 1890s.

DeWolfe, Jerome, Dakota Sioux descendant of the brave who took the DeWolf name after Doctor DeWolf was killed; *Interview with Gene and Ann Erb at his South Dakota home, Oct. 8, 2001.*

Dodd, Carolyn, widow of Verne A. Dodd Jr., Frances J. DeWolf Dodd's grandson. *Telephone interview with Gene Erb, Jan. 14, 2002.*

Dodd, Doctor Verne A.; Luce, Edward S. *Letters of correspondence in 1941 re Dodd's donations to Custer Battlefield National Cemetery of Doctor James M. DeWolf's 1876 diary and letters.* Little Bighorn Battlefield National Monument archives. Crow Agency, MT.

Fort Totten Medical History Log, official daily reports of activities at the post. Fort Totten, 1875-1876.

Neal, Beverly, great-granddaughter of Frances Jane "Fannie" DeWolf Dodd; *Telephone interview with Gene Erb, Jan. 14, 2002, followed by meetings with Gene and Ann Erb in Ohio and Arizona.*

Gene Erb is also the author of *A Plague of Hunger* based on two award-winning newspaper series, one focusing on the migration of jobs from Iowa to Mexico and the other examining world hunger issues. A former U.S. Navy pilot, Mr. Erb was a reporter and editor with the *Des Moines Register* and *Tribune* from 1974 through 2000. He has a bachelor's degree from Iowa State University and a master's degree in journalism from the University of Missouri.

Ann DeWolf Erb was a librarian at Iowa State University for five years and then an analyst, manager and officer at an Iowa insurance company through 2000. She has a bachelor's degree from the University of West Florida and a master's degree in library science from the University of Rhode Island. She is a distant cousin of Dr. James Madison DeWolf.

The authors live in Iowa.

LaVergne, TN USA
23 June 2010
187133LV00004B/4/P